A note on BLACKWATER

Michael McDowell has taken on a remarkable challenge with a novel the scope of BLACKWATER.

His work has ranged from the contemporary novel of horror set in the American South (THE AMULET, COLD MOON OVER BABYLON, and THE ELEMENTALS) to the extravagantly detailed novel of America in another time (GILDED NEEDLES and KATIE).

His fullest powers are mustered now in his six-part novel, BLACKWATER, which Peter Straub, author of GHOST STORY, says "looks like Michael McDowell's best yet... it seduces and intrigues... makes us impatient for the next volume." Straub says McDowell is "beyond any trace of doubt, one of the absolutely best writers of horror"; Stephen King calls McDowell "the finest writer of paperback originals in America"; and the *Washington Post* promises "Cliffhangers guaranteed."

MICHAEL McDOWELL'S
BLACKWATER:

III

THE
HOUSE

◆ **AVON**
PUBLISHERS OF BARD, CAMELOT, DISCUS AND FLARE BOOKS

BLACKWATER: III THE HOUSE is an original publication of Avon Books. This work has never before appeared in book form.

AVON BOOKS
A division of
The Hearst Corporation
959 Eighth Avenue
New York, New York 10019

First Avon Printing, March, 1983

Our story 'til now...

Following her mysterious appearance during the flood of 1919 in Perdido, Alabama, Elinor Dammert marries into the town's leading family, the Caskeys. After surrendering her first child, Miriam, to her possessive mother-in-law, Mary-Love, Elinor settles down to a contented married life with Oscar, her happiness marred only by the town's plans to build a levee for protection against future flooding. Although Elinor insists that no flood will ever again come to Perdido while she is alive, an engineer named Early Haskew is brought in to supervise the project.

To spite Elinor, Mary-Love invites Early to stay with her and her spinster daughter, Sister, who promptly begins scheming behind her mother's back to marry the engineer. Sister is aided in her efforts by the occult conniving of Ivey, the family cook.

Elinor, still unhappy about the levee but tolerant of Early and Sister's marriage if only because it makes Mary-Love so upset, gives birth to a second child, Frances. Frances will be her child as Miriam never could, for it is apparent from the very beginning that Frances shares Elinor's mysterious otherworldly heritage.

James Caskey, Oscar's widowed uncle, is paid a visit by his penniless sister-in-law, Queenie, and her two children, Malcolm and Lucille. Queenie claims to be escaping from her husband, Carl, and clearly wishes to take refuge with the Caskeys. Although she at first appears to be a conniving opportunist, when her husband shows up and rapes her, she is accepted, with various degrees of sympathy, into the Caskey family, with Elinor as her prime sponsor.

By the end of THE LEVEE, Volume II of the BLACKWATER saga, Elinor has reconciled herself to the damming up of her beloved Perdido's waters by dint of a private and terrible sacrifice.

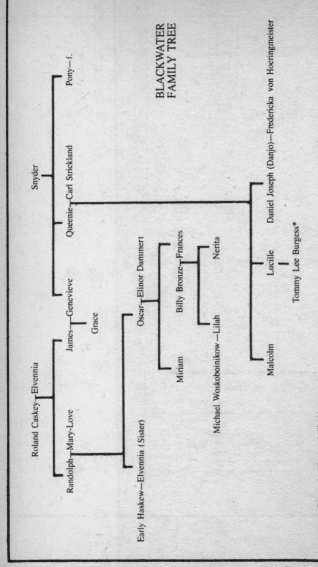

BLACKWATER
FAMILY TREE

*Note: Tommy Lee Burgess is illegitimate.

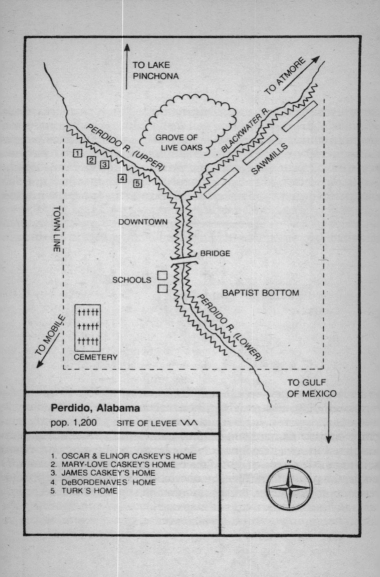

TO LAKE
PINCHONA

TO ATMORE

GROVE OF
LIVE OAKS

BLACKWATER R.

PERDIDO R. (UPPER)

SAWMILLS

1
2
3
4
5

TOWN LINE

DOWNTOWN

BRIDGE

SCHOOLS

BAPTIST BOTTOM

TO MOBILE

†††††
†††††
†††††

CEMETERY

PERDIDO R. (LOWER)

TO GULF
OF MEXICO

N

Perdido, Alabama

pop. 1,200   SITE OF LEVEE ∨∨∨

1. OSCAR & ELINOR CASKEY'S HOME
2. MARY-LOVE CASKEY'S HOME
3. JAMES CASKEY'S HOME
4. DeBORDENAVE'S HOME
5. TURK'S HOME

CHAPTER 28

~~~~~~

Miriam and Frances

Frances and Miriam Caskey were sisters born scarcely a year apart. They lived next door to each other in houses that were no more than a few dozen yards distant. Yet, so little commerce was maintained between their respective households that when they did meet—on the rare occasions of Caskey state—the sisters were shy and mistrustful.

While Miriam was the elder by only about twelve months, in maturity she seemed to outdistance her sister by years. Reared in the house with her grandmother Mary-Love Caskey and her aunt Sister Haskew, until Sister and her husband moved away, Miriam had been fondled and coddled and pampered for every waking moment of her seven years. This indulgence had become more marked since 1926, when Sister, at last disgusted beyond endurance by her mother's interferences and meddlesomeness, persuaded her husband to move to Mississippi. Mary-Love and Miriam had been left alone in their rambling house, and were one another's company and solace. It was a common remark in Perdido that Miriam was just like Mary-Love, and not a bit like her own mother, who lived right next door and saw Miriam less often than she saw the hairdresser.

Miriam, like all the Caskeys, was slender and tall, and Mary-Love saw to it that she was always dressed in the best of childhood fashion. Miriam was a neat, fastidious child; she talked nearly constantly, but never loudly. Her conversation turned mostly on what things she had seen in the possession of others, what things she had recently acquired, what things she still coveted. Miriam had her own room, with furniture specially bought for it. She herself had picked out the miniature rolltop desk from the showroom of a furniture store in Mobile. She loved its multitude of tiny drawers. Now every one of those tiny drawers was filled with things: buttons, lace, pieces of cheap jewelry, pencils, small porcelain figurines of dogs, spangles, ribbons, scraps of colored paper, and other such pretty detritus that could be gathered up in a household rich in worldly goods. Miriam occupied herself for hours on end quietly looking through these items, rearranging them, stacking them, counting them, making records of them in a neat ledger, and scheming to get more.

The possessions, however, that afforded Miriam Caskey greatest pleasure were those she was not allowed to keep in her room. These were the diamonds and emeralds and pearls that her grandmother presented to her on Christmas, on her birthday, and on a few otherwise run-of-the-mill days in between, and then hid away in a safety-deposit box in Mobile. "You are too young to keep this jewelry yourself," Mary-Love said to her beloved granddaughter, "but you should always remember that it's yours."

Miriam had a confused view of adulthood and wasn't sure that she would ever reach that exalted state. While she couldn't be certain that the jewels would ever be given over to her direct possession, this didn't matter in the least to her. Thoughts of those jewels, in the distant, locked, silent safety-deposit box in Mobile always entered her mind before going to sleep every night and seemed almost to make up for the lullaby her real mother would never sing to her.

Frances Caskey was very different. While Miriam was energetic and robust and strung together with a wiry nervous tension, Frances seemed to have a tenuous hold on her body and her health. Frances caught colds and fevers with dismaying ease; she developed allergies and brief undiagnosed illnesses with the frequency with which other children scraped their knees. She was timid in general, and would no more have thought it her prerogative to be jealous of her sister or her sister's possessions than she would have thought it her right to declare herself Queen of All the Americas.

Frances spent every day with Zaddie Sapp, shyly carrying and fetching in the kitchen, or following Zaddie about the house, sitting quietly in a corner with her feet carefully raised off the floor while Zaddie swept and dusted and polished. Frances was well behaved, never out of sorts, patient in sickness, willing—even eager—to perform any act or task delegated to her. Her self-effacement was so pronounced that her grandmother—on those rare occasions when Mary-Love saw her—would shake her by the shoulders, and cry, "Perk up, child! Where's your gumption? You act like there's somebody waiting to jump out from behind the door and grab you!"

Every weekday morning, Frances would slip out onto the front porch on the second floor of the house and surreptitiously watch for her sister to leave for school. Miriam, always in a freshly starched dress and nicely polished shoes, would come out with her books and seat herself carefully in the back of the

11

Packard. Miss Mary-Love would come out onto the porch, and call out, "Bray, come drive Miriam to school!" Bray would stand up from his gardening, brush off his hands, and drive away with Miriam, who always sat as still and composed and stately as if she were on her way to be presented to the Queen of England. In the afternoon, when Frances saw Bray driving off again, Frances would station herself to witness the return of her sister, as starched and polished and unruffled as when she had departed in the morning.

Frances wasn't jealous of her sister, but she was in awe of her, and she treasured memories of the few occasions when Miriam had spoken a kind word to her. Clasped around her neck, Frances wore the thin gold chain and locket that Miriam had given her the previous Christmas. It didn't matter one bit that afterward, Miriam had whispered to her, "Grandmama picked it out. Ivey found a box. They put my name on it, but I never even saw it. I wouldn't have spent all that money on you."

In the autumn of 1928, Frances was eager to enter the first grade. She occupied herself relentlessly with the question of whether she would be allowed to ride with Miriam and Bray to school every morning. She dared not put the question to her parents directly for fear the answer would be no. The thought of being allowed to sit beside Miriam in the back seat of the Packard made Frances quiver in expectation. She daydreamed of intimacy with Miriam.

When the first day of school finally arrived, Zaddie put Frances into her best dress. Oscar kissed his daughter, and Elinor told her to be very good and very smart. Frances went expectantly out the front door alone—it seemed for the very first time in her whole life—only to see her grandmother's Packard roll off down the street with Bray behind the wheel.

Starched and polished Miriam sat all alone in the back.

Frances drooped onto the steps and wept.

Oscar marched across to his mother's house, entered without knocking, and angrily said to Mary-Love, "Mama, how in creation could you let Bray drive off and leave poor little Frances sitting on the front steps?"

"Oh?" said Mary-Love, with the appearance of surprise, "was Frances intending on riding with Miriam?"

"Well, you know she was, Mama. It's her first day at school. Miriam could have shown her where to go."

"Miriam couldn't have done that," returned Mary-Love hastily. "She might have been late. I cain't let Miriam be late on her first day at school."

Oscar sighed. "Miriam wouldn't have been late, Mama. Poor Frances is just sitting on the steps, weeping bitter tears."

"I cain't help that," replied Mary-Love, unperturbed.

"Well, tell me this, Mama," Oscar went on, "are you gone let my little girl ride with Bray and Miriam from now on?"

Mary-Love pondered this a moment, then replied at last, grudgingly: "If she insists on it, Oscar. But only if she's out there waiting in the car when Miriam comes out of this house. I'm not gone have black marks against Miriam because Frances cain't get herself dressed on time."

"Mama," said Oscar, "are you forgetting that I pay half of Bray's salary?"

"Are you forgetting it's *my* automobile?"

Oscar was furious. On this first day of his daughter's scholastic career, he drove Frances to school himself, showed her to the proper room, and introduced her to her teacher. At dinnertime, he told his wife what Mary-Love had said.

"Oscar," said Elinor, "your mama treats Frances like the dirt under her feet. I hate to think how many diamonds she has bought for Miriam. I hate to think what that child is worth in rubies and pearls alone. That locket they sent over here at Christmas must have cost all of seventy-five cents. I'm not going to have Miss Mary-Love do us any favors. We are not going to allow Frances to ride in that car—not once. People in town will *see* how Miss Mary-Love treats her own granddaughter!"

Frances, who had enjoyed such high hopes for closeness with her sister, knew no intimacy at all. Every morning, Zaddie took Frances's hand and walked her all the way to school—in fact, all the way to the door of the schoolroom—and left her there. Sometimes Bray and Miriam would pass them in the road, but Miriam wouldn't even wave or nod to her sister. On the playground, Miriam would not play in any game in which her sister took part. "I'm in the second grade," said Miriam to her sister on a rare occasion that she suffered herself to speak to her, "and I know *this* much more than you!" As Miriam spread her arms to their widest extent, Frances was crushed by the sense of her own inferiority.

Mary-Love's neglect of her second grandchild was not lost on Miriam, who had grown actively to despise her sister. She was embarrassed by Frances's shyness, her inferior wardrobe, her dependence on Zaddie Sapp for companionship and affection, her lack of knowledge concerning real jewels, real crystal, and good china.

Miriam's feelings about Frances were intensified during the first weeks of December, when the first and second grades of the Perdido Elementary School began their Christmas seal campaigns. Miriam thought that selling door-to-door like a man with vacuum cleaners was an activity beneath her. She decided only to repeat her previous year's performance and sell a few dollar's worth of the seals to

Mary-Love and to Queenie, so as not simply to have a zero placed next to her name on the special chalkboards set up in the school hallway.

Frances, however, took the business very seriously—in her small way—and set out to sell as many of the seals as she could; her teacher had told her it was a worthy cause. With Oscar's permission, Frances paid a visit to the mill and went through the offices approaching all the workers. Frances was so diffident, so slight, and so charming in her own way that everyone bought a large quantity. Her great-uncle James Caskey and his daughter Grace then purchased more seals than all the millworkers combined. Before she knew it, Frances had sold more than anyone else on the first grade board.

Miriam was astonished and humiliated by Frances's success. Suddenly nothing in the world was more important than beating her sister at selling Christmas seals. Mary-Love, not understanding the importance of the matter to her granddaughter, resisted buying any more than she could use. So Miriam went next door to James and to Grace, who claimed that they would like to oblige her, but were all bought out. Miriam went to the mill, under James's aegis, but everyone there had already opened his purse to Frances. Miriam even swallowed enough pride to knock upon a few doors, but since it was late in the campaign, everyone who might have been persuaded to buy had already bought his seals.

In despair, she went to her grandmother and explained her dilemma. Contrary to Miriam's expectations, Mary-Love was by no means angry with her. "You mean to tell me, Miriam darling, that that little girl next door is gone beat you out—and you're in the second grade and she's in the first?"

"James and Grace bought so many, Grandmama. And they wouldn't buy a single seal from me!"

"They wouldn't? And they bought from Frances?"

Miriam nodded glumly. "I hate Frances!"

15

"I am *not* gone let Elinor Caskey's child beat you out. How much has she sold so far? Do you know?"

"Thirty-five dollars and thirty-five cents."

"And how much have *you* sold?"

"Three dollars and ten cents."

"And when is the contest over?"

"Day after tomorrow."

"All right, then," said Mary-Love, lowering her voice. "I tell you what, Miriam. After school tomorrow, you go find out if Frances has sold any more. Then you bring me her total, you understand?"

And on the final day of the sale of the Christmas seals, Miriam Caskey brought in forty-two dollars, an astounding sum considering that everybody in Perdido had drawersful of the things by now, and that up to that point Miriam had brought in no more than three dollars. When her teacher asked her who in the world had bought so many, Miriam replied, "I knocked on every door in town. I near 'bout walked my legs off."

The Caskey sisters came in first and second in the contest, but Miriam beat her sister by almost seven dollars. Miriam won a Bible with six illustrations in color and all of Jesus's words printed in red. Frances got a box of Whitman's candy.

After the presentation of the awards, Frances opened her box of candy and offered it to her sister, telling her to take as much of it as she wanted. But as Miriam bit into the largest piece she could find, liquid cherry squirted out over the front of her starched dress. "Ugh!" she cried, "it's your fault, Frances! Look at me now!" And with a fling of her hand she knocked the box out of Frances's grasp, spilling all the chocolates into the dirt of the schoolyard.

The rivalry that appeared to exist between the estranged sisters was emblematic of the much greater rivalry that had risen between Elinor Caskey and

16

her mother-in-law, Mary-Love. Through those two little girls was played out, in distorting miniature, the passion that characterized the relationship of their mother and grandmother. Mary-Love was the undisputed head of the Caskey family, having acceded to that position upon the death of her husband many years before. No one had challenged her authority before the arrival in Perdido of Elinor Dammert. With single-minded energy that had matched Mary-Love's own best weapons, Elinor had arranged to be courted by and married to Mary-Love's only son, Oscar.

The two women had quite different styles. Elinor didn't have Mary-Love's bluster; her ways were more insidious. Elinor bided her time; her strokes were quick, clean, and always unexpected. Mary-Love knew this, and in the last few years she had grown restive, as if waiting for the blow that would topple her. Mary-Love's antipathy toward her daughter-in-law had grown strident and unbecoming. Perdido talked, and the talk was always against Mary-Love. It was one thing to disapprove of a son's wife; it was another to make that dislike so widely known. Mary-Love eventually had come to see that it simply would not do to give Elinor battle directly. Elinor remained cool, always seeming to contemplate the skirmish beyond the one that hotly occupied Mary-Love. Elinor gave way strategically, and then flashed her sword just at the moment that Mary-Love was raising her arm to claim victory. Like a palsied general, Mary-Love decided to retire from the field, but did not give up the war.

In her granddaughter Miriam, Mary-Love had an eager, conscienceless, and bloodthirsty little soldier. And Frances, Elinor's representative, was a sickly enemy—timid and weaponless. A skirmish between the sisters would incontestably give the victory to Mary-Love's side. Daily, Mary-Love wrapped up her granddaughter in her prettiest dresses and shiniest

17

shoes, kissed her on the cheek, and whispered, "Give no quarter..."

There was no satisfaction, however, for either Miriam or her grandmother, in these easy victories, because Frances didn't fight at all. She looked around with puzzlement, not even realizing that she had wandered onto a field of battle. If she had seen fit, Elinor might have instructed her daughter in matters of combat and strategy, but Elinor had done nothing. Perdido talked about the two little girls, as before they had talked about Elinor and Mary-Love. Perdido's conclusion was that Miriam was disagreeable and much too big for her britches, and that Frances was as sweet as sweet could be. *That* said something about the two households in which the children were reared.

Thus, by sending out her emissary unarmed, unprepared, and even ignorant of the fact that war had been declared, Elinor had gained the day. How long would it be, Mary-Love wondered uncomfortably, before Elinor stormed the citadel itself, and claimed supremacy over the Caskey clan? Why had she not done it yet? If she waited for a sign or portent, what was it? How might Mary-Love prepare herself against that inevitable day? And when the two women came to do battle, what casualties would be borne bloody and broken from the field of conflict?

CHAPTER 29

The Coins in Queenie's Pocket

Queenie Strickland, after a tumultuous appearance in Perdido six years earlier, had settled down. She and her children had taken on a greater identity than mere penurious offshoots of the Caskeys. It was generally known in Perdido that Queenie's third child Daniel Joseph—universally called Danjo from the hour of his birth—was the result of a rape committed on Queenie by her estranged husband. It had also become generally known that Danjo's father was no good, that Queenie wanted no reconciliation, and that Danjo was much better off growing up without even having seen so much as a photograph of his father.

Queenie had gained a reputation in Perdido of being a sponger. The designation, though accurate, was repugnant to her. Shortly after the birth of her third child, she announced to James that she intended to seek employment. James, not wishing anyone else in town shouldering a burden he considered his own, appointed her his personal secretary. His sense of responsibility toward his unfortunate and indigent sister-in-law was greater than his doubt as to the extent of her clerical abilities and his misgivings as to what their daily propinquity at the mill office would be like.

In the summer of 1925 James had sent Queenie to Pensacola to take a typing course at the mechanics college there and thereby gave her a much needed rest from the demands of Malcolm, Lucille, and little Danjo. James would not have these rambunctious children in his own home, filled as it was with much that was fragile and valuable, but instead sent Grace over to Queenie's to care for them there.

When Queenie returned, she was proficient at the typewriter, and in a short time she became indispensable to her brother-in-law, providing pencils, advice, coffee, a sympathetic ear, and freedom from obtrusive callers. She proved her worth, both in her official and private capacities, far beyond anything James Caskey could have imagined, and Queenie quickly came to know everything there was to know concerning the running of the Caskey mill. Since Queenie was close to Elinor, Elinor in turn learned what little her husband had not already told her. Queenie had long before been trained as Elinor's spy, and she retained that position now.

Queenie's intimacy with James Caskey and Elinor helped her to feel more secure and thus she became calmer. During her first year or so in Perdido she had not hesitated to employ a gushing hypocrisy to get what she wanted; she had mooned over James's crystal, echoed Elinor's decrying of the levee construction, and nodded vigorously at the list of the wrongs Mary-Love perceived had been made against her. She learned how quickly all this had been seen through by the Caskeys, and now she took great care to examine her own feelings on any matter and always expressed those feelings cautiously. Honesty in this case proved by far the best policy, though Queenie employed truthfulness exactly as she had employed hypocrisy—as a means to an end, and not as a thing to be appreciated for itself.

Although her principal struggle had apparently been won—Carl Strickland remaining mercifully absent from the scene—Queenie experienced her share of trials. These usually involved her children, and centered mostly on Malcolm, her eldest. He was ten, in the fourth grade, and prone to many minor mischiefs. He broke windows in abandoned houses, pocketed small items at the Ben Franklin store, and went swimming in the upper Perdido, where he was in some danger of being sucked down to the junction and drowned. He threw sand through the screens of Miss Elinor's kitchen in order to annoy Zaddie Sapp. He knocked his teacher's plants off the windowsill for the pleasure of hearing the pots smash on the pavement below. He threw potatoes at little girls. He stole his friends' marbles. He was loud and raucous. He insulted every Negro child who crossed his path, and he continued to indulge every opportunity of punching his brother and his sister in the stomach. Every time the telephone rang in James's office Queenie feared it would be another call complaining of Malcolm's behavior.

Eight-year-old Lucille was easier on her mother's nerves, but still caused Queenie a fair amount of grief. Lucille was sneaky, although Queenie would never voice this appraisal of her daughter, even to Elinor. Lucille lied when it suited her purpose. Lucille couldn't be tucked into bed without her whispering in her mother's ear some wrong she had suffered at her brother's hand. If she decided she needed a new pair of shoes, she wasn't above climbing the levee—against all orders—and deliberately kicking one of her best patent leathers into the muddy

21

water of the Perdido and therewith validating her desire.

For the third child, four-year-old Danjo, Queenie held great hope. He was remarkably different from his siblings; he was everything they were not. He was calm, quiet, truthful, pleasant, and well behaved. It was as if his whole being had been sobered by an intuitive knowledge of the unhappy circumstances of his conception. He was the only one of Queenie's children James would allow into his house, the only one Mary-Love would stoop down and kiss, and the only one Elinor invited to sit beside her on the swing. Danjo acted as if he lived only by the generous sufferance of the whole world, and that if he performed any untoward act or spoke any unsuitable word he would be picked up by one hundred hands and mercilessly hurled into the river. It was generally considered a point in Danjo's favor that neither his sister nor his brother liked him. During his nightly bath, Queenie generally found some new bruise or pinch mark that had been surreptitiously administered by either Malcolm or Lucille. The teachers in the school sighed in relief as Malcolm passed on up a grade, bore with stony resignation the presence of untrustworthy Lucille, and all sighed the same thought: *Lord, I can hardly wait till I get that precious child Danjo Strickland! After Malcolm and Lucille I will have earned him!*

Of her husband's doings, whereabouts, and condition Queenie had heard absolutely nothing. She thought there was a strong possibility that since he had not showed up again he was being prevented from doing so by the interposition of iron bars and prison walls. Whatever the case, Queenie knew that she would be protected from Carl by James and Oscar, who had come to her aid before, but still she always feared being taken by surprise. At night her house was locked tighter than any other home in Perdido, and an intruder might have got into the

Perdido bank with greater ease at the same hour. When Queenie sat on her front porch she always had an escape route should she see Carl come walking down the street. Every strange automobile pulling up before the house caused her trepidation. She dreaded the postman because he might be delivering a message from Carl. She hated to pick up the telephone at home for fear Carl's voice would greet her on the other end.

But all her precautions were of no avail; when Carl did return, Queenie was wholly unprepared for the hour and the manner of his arrival.

He was simply sitting on her porch one afternoon when she came home from work. Danjo was held an unhappy captive on his father's lap. Lucille and Malcolm stood inside the safety of the house, wildly gesticulating to their mother through the screen door.

"Ma!" cried Malcolm in a stage whisper as she came up the steps, "we locked the door. We wouldn't let him inside."

"Hey, Queenie," said Carl softly, "how you?"

He was wearing a suit, and looked uncomfortable in it.

Queenie suddenly felt herself borne down with the weight of the world. She realized how happy she had been for the past five years, how she hadn't known a moment of *real* disquietude, had never gone without money or company or—she was astonished to think it for the first time—respect. With the reappearance of her husband in Perdido, all of that instantly vanished.

"What you doing back here, Carl?"

"Came to see you, Queenie. Where'd this here boy come from?"

Queenie didn't answer.

"Been lonesome, Queenie?" he asked with a leer.

"No," she returned. "Not one single little bit." She waved Malcolm and Lucille away from the door. They retreated a few steps, but returned almost immediately as soon as their mother's back was turned. Queenie seated herself in the rocker across from Carl. "Give me my baby," she said.

"Whose baby is he?" said Carl, not letting go of Danjo.

"He's yours."

"You sure, Queenie? Maybe you made a mistake."

"I didn't make any mistake. Danjo, come here."

Carl said, "Kiss your daddy."

Danjo wriggled out of Carl's grasp and fled to his mother's lap.

"Where you been?" asked Queenie. She didn't look at her husband, but stared out across the street.

"Here and there."

"What pen were you in?"

"Tallahassee." He grinned.

"What for this time?"

"Never you mind."

Queenie was silent a moment, then she said, "Carl, I want you to go away. Me and Malcolm and Lucille and Danjo don't need you. We don't want you."

"I cain't desert my family, Queenie. What kind of man you take me for?"

"I don't intend to argue," said Queenie with weariness and despair pervading her voice. "I just want you to go away from this town and never come back again."

"Oh, Queenie, you cain't get rid of me. I'm your husband. I got legal rights. I got my children here that need me. That Malcolm's a fine one, I tell you. That Lucille's a little doll! And this boy Danjo, I'm gone help you bring him up right."

Queenie stood and headed toward the door. Carl rose quickly and followed her.

"Unhook the screen," Queenie said to Malcolm. She was carrying Danjo and shifted him in her arms.

"I don't want him in here!" screamed Lucille.

"Baby girl!" cried Carl.

"Unhook the screen," Queenie repeated.

Malcolm sullenly did so. Queenie slipped inside; Carl followed her in.

"Have you got a bag?" Queenie asked.

"Out on the porch, Queenie. Didn't you see it?"

"I saw it." She reached in her purse and took out five dollars. "Go take it over to the Osceola."

He snatched the five dollars from her. "I can use this, but I tell you, I ain't gone waste it on no hotel. I'm gone stay right here."

"No," said Queenie.

"Yes," he said, taking her arm and squeezing it hard.

Queenie's neck stretched with the pain, but she said nothing.

Carl slipped the five dollars into his pocket and let go of his wife's arm. "Queenie, I sure am thirsty," he said in a light, conversational voice. "You think you could fix me some iced tea?"

Carl sat down on the sofa and motioned his children over to him. Queenie looked at her husband, but there was no intelligible message in her gaze. She went into the kitchen, calling after her, "Lucille, I need some help."

While Malcolm and Danjo sat uncomfortably on either side of their father and answered the questions put to them, Queenie in the kitchen whispered to her daughter, "Go out the back way. Run over to Elinor's and tell her your daddy has come back. She'll know what to do."

Lucille took off immediately, allowing the back door to slam shut behind her. A moment later Carl pushed open the kitchen door. "Was that my baby girl going somewhere?"

"I sent her to tell the Caskeys that you'd come back."

"So they can come greet me, tell me how glad they are to see me back in Perdido."

"No," said Queenie. "So they can get you out of

25

town. On a rail. Tied to the back of a mule. Floating down the river on the back of a log."

"They got me out once, sugar, but I wasn't smart. I learned me a few things in the Tallahassee pen. Now I turned smart. I'm your lawful wedded husband, Queenie, and I'm gone stay around and help raise up my precious babies. I sent that boy Malcolm out on the porch and he's gone bring in my bag. Those Caskeys aren't gone be able to do a thing. I'm here to stay, Queenie. I look around, what do I see? I see a nice house. I see my babies and my wife. I see plenty to eat. Is there one reason on earth why I should go away?"

Queenie didn't reply. She handed him a glass of iced tea and walked out of the kitchen and back into the living room. Danjo sat on the sofa, weeping softly.

But it wasn't all that easy to get rid of Queenie's husband. Oscar went over to speak to Carl and Carl said, "Who's gone throw me out of town? Where's your gun? You gone shoot me? Where's your lawman? He gone arrest me for visiting my wife? He gone put me in jail for bouncing my little boy up and down on my knee?"

Aubrey Wiggins had been sheriff the first time Carl Strickland had showed up in Perdido. Wiggins assisted Oscar in driving the unwanted man out of town. Now Aubrey was dead, and his place had been taken by Charley Key. Charley was Perdido's youngest sheriff ever. He was hotheaded and quick to take offense. He was particularly chary of doing favors or of having favors done for him. It was thought generally that in a few years he would see the light and then things would be accomplished with the ease and smoothness that had characterized his predecessor's administration. But for right now, Sheriff Key wasn't listening when Oscar came to him and said, "Mr. Key, I need you to back me up with Queenie Strickland's husband. He's no good and he ought to be run out of town."

"What's he done?"

"He's bothering her."

"How's he bothering her, Mr. Caskey?"

"He's moved in on her."

"Aren't they married?"

"They are."

"Then what's to stop him? A husband and a wife ought pretty much to be together. That's about the way I've always heard it."

"James and I want him to leave. He's making Queenie unhappy, and we care a great deal for Queenie, Mr. Key."

"I know Queenie Strickland," replied the sheriff. "What I know of her, I like. I haven't met her husband. Where's he been?"

"Florida pen," said Oscar in a low voice. This wasn't general knowledge in Perdido, and his tone of conspiracy was a plea for the sheriff to keep the information to himself.

"What for?"

"Don't know. But probably just about anything you care to name."

"Is he out free and clear?"

"He says he is."

"Then there's nothing I can do."

"He's making Queenie *real* unhappy, Mr. Key."

"Lots of unhappy marriages. I cain't always be stepping in between a husband and a wife. Tell you what I will do, though. I'll call up Tallahassee and make sure he hasn't escaped. If he's escaped from the pen, then I'll go after him. If he hasn't, then there's not one thing in the world I can do, Mr. Caskey."

Sheriff Key wanted to show Oscar and the other Caskeys that their prominence in Perdido brought them no special treatment from the forces of order and justice. This Oscar understood, but he knew it

27

was Queenie who would suffer on account of the sheriff's procedural niceties. Oscar decided not to argue with the sheriff any longer. He returned home to where his wife and Queenie were waiting on the porch and related the disappointing news.

Elinor was incensed, but her anger could not persuade Mr. Key, and without Mr. Key nothing at all could be done.

Queenie said to Oscar and Elinor: "That man made my life miserable in Nashville, and he's gone ruin my life here, too. You know what it's gone be like to come home from work every day just knowing he's sitting there on the porch, wanting to know what I'm gone fix him for supper?"

"Oscar," said Elinor, "why don't you just run over there with your gun and shoot him? Queenie and I will wait here till you get back."

"Elinor, I'm not gone shoot Carl Strickland. Queenie, you think if I offered him money, he'd go away? That must be why he's here, right? 'Cause you've got a job and a house and all?"

"Won't work," sighed Queenie. "James offered him two hundred dollars a month if he'd go live two states away. Carl wouldn't take it. Carl said he wanted to be near his 'darling babies.' I tell y'all, I am afraid for those children. It hasn't been easy raising them on my own. Poor old Malcolm sure hasn't come out the way I wanted him to. He gets in a lot of trouble already. I hate to think what Carl is gone do to 'em!"

"Oscar, I really do think you ought to go over and shoot that man!"

"You want me in jail, Elinor? That's where I'd be. You'd have to come visit me up in the Atmore pen. I'd be out in the hot sun digging potatoes all day. That's what murderers do up there in Atmore."

Nothing could be done. Oscar's threats remained vague without the force of the law behind them. Carl had served his sentence in full for holding up a pharmacy in DeFuniak Springs and pistol-whipping the proprietor. He could now be accused of doing nothing that was against the law. He wasn't working. What need had he of employment when his wife worked and pulled down good money, when the house was hers free and clear, and when there was food on the table and clothing on his children's backs?

Queenie was miserable. Whenever James came into her office, he'd find her attempting to cover up the fact that she'd been crying. Kindly, he always attempted to persuade his distraught sister-in-law that Carl's residence was only temporary. "When the time comes, I'll up my offer. And one day, I'll name his price. Soon enough, Queenie, he'll be moving on."

Carl had taken over his wife's bedroom. Queenie slept on the sofa in the living room or sometimes with Lucille.

How Carl spent his days no one was certain. After James picked Queenie up in the morning, Carl often took his wife's car and drove off somewhere. Someone told Elinor she had seen him at the racetrack in Cantonement. Someone else saw him lunching off oysters in a restaurant on the Mobile pier. He was seen on the front porch of the house with the red light in Baptist Bottom. But he was always found sitting on the front porch by the time that Queenie returned from work, saying, "Hey, Queenie, what's for supper? I'm starved to death!"

One evening Queenie came home to discover that Carl had a large bruise around his left eye. She didn't ask how it had come about, uttered no word of sympathy, didn't warn him against becoming involved in possibly more serious altercations. "I bet you wish I'd gotten my whole head knocked off, don't you?" said Carl with his customary leer. "I bet that, on the whole, you wouldn't much mind the state of widowhood, would you?"

"I think I could bear up," replied Queenie blandly.

"I bet you've got my coffin all picked out!"

Queenie reached into the pocket of her dress and drew out two coins.

"You see these quarters?" she asked.

"I see 'em."

"They're for you."

"Give 'em here, then." He reached out for the coins, but Queenie snatched them away.

"No. They're special."

"How special?"

"Ivey Sapp gave 'em to me when I was over at Mary-Love's yesterday."

"That fat nigger girl? Why was she giving you money?"

"She told me she got 'em special for me," Queenie went on with a smile that was very rare to her since Carl had come back to town. "She told me to save these quarters for the ferryman."

"What ferryman?"

"Ivey told me to always keep 'em with me. So when you're laid out dead and cold, I've got these two silver quarters to close your eyes with. And that's what you'll have to buy your ticket to hell with."

Carl's grin faded. He reached out and swiped for the coins, but wasn't quick enough and Queenie dropped them, with a little metallic clatter, back into her pocket.

CHAPTER 30

Danjo

In the eight years since the death of Genevieve Caskey, the widower James Caskey and his daughter Grace had remained in perpetual harmony in the house next door to Mary-Love. It was wondered in Perdido whether any father and any daughter, anywhere on the face of the earth, got along as well as did James and Grace. James would have done anything to make his little girl happy. Grace had declared, as a high school senior, that she would never, under any circumstances, be persuaded to leave her father's roof.

"No!" he cried. "You cain't stay here with me and rot, darling. You got to go to school!"

"I don't," returned Grace. "I know plenty. I'm gone be salutatorian this year, Daddy."

"Doesn't matter. You ought to go away to school. You ought to get out of Perdido for a while."

"I'm happy here. I'm *perfectly* happy, Daddy. I've got all my friends here." Grace ran with a pack of girls in her class and the class behind hers. They were all on terms of great intimacy, and they never had fights. "Besides, Daddy, who would take care of you?"

"About fifty million people would take care of me. Are you forgetting Mary-Love next door? Are you forgetting Elinor? Have you thought of Queenie? You think Queenie would let anything happen to me?"

"Queenie has her hands full with Carl," Grace pointed out. "And Elinor and Miss Mary-Love spend all their time raising little girls and fighting with each other."

"The point is," her father went on, "you ought to go to school. You ought to get out in the world, and meet the man who's gone make you happy."

"He doesn't exist!"

"He does. There's somebody for everybody, sweetheart! There's some man just waiting out there to fix you up with a perfect marriage."

"I don't believe it. I look around me, Daddy, what do I see? I see you and poor old Mama—"

"That was *my* mistake."

"—and I see Queenie and Carl. You think I'm gone start looking under bushel baskets for a husband?"

"What about Elinor and Oscar? They're happy."

"They're the exception, Daddy."

"Well, you could be an exception too, darling. I'm sure you would be. So I'm just not gone let you stay in Perdido, thinking you are doing me one bit of good. Darling, I love you to death, but let me tell you something—"

"What?"

"—I've had just about as much of your company as I can take!"

Grace laughed aloud at her father's patent lie.

"I want you out of this house!" His attempt at sternness was belied by seventeen years of singular indulgence.

"What if I say no?"

32

"I will have Roxie *sweep* you out. I will hook the screens behind you. If you don't go away to college, Grace, I'm not gone love you anymore."

Each was determined to make sacrifices for the other's benefit and comfort. Though Grace desperately longed to attend college, she told her father her sole desire was to remain with him in Perdido. Though James knew he would be desolate without her, he told his daughter he was weary of her company, and only wished she *would* go to Tennessee. For several weeks, father and daughter continued to argue until at last Grace gave in. She realized what pleasure would accrue to her father in being abandoned in the cause of her personal happiness. So Grace made plans, though convinced that without her, James would be lonely and miserable. She was to attend Vanderbilt in September.

And so, during the hottest part of August of 1929, Grace and James drove up through Alabama to Nashville, Tennessee, looked over the campus, were introduced to the president of the college, and chose the room Grace would inhabit. They went shopping for Grace's wardrobe, and purchased enough to clothe the entire co-ed freshman class. They went around to all the jewelry, gift, and antique shops, and James indulged himself in the purchase of any number of fragile, pretty, utterly useless items that would be jammed into bursting closets back home.

On their final evening together, James took his daughter to Nashville's best restaurant. He gave her an envelope stuffed with five-dollar bills, and said, "Darling, if you need anything, pick up the telephone and call me, you hear? Send a telegram. Whatever it is, I'll get it up here to you."

"When can I come home?"

"Anytime. I'll borrow Bray and he'll meet you in Atmore. You always keep enough money for a train ticket, you hear?"

"Daddy, I'm gone miss you so much!"

"You think I'm not gone miss you?"

"You said you weren't."

"I was lying. I don't know what I'm gone do without you. You're my baby. If I could I'd keep you with me, but that wouldn't do either of us any good. When I was your age, I was living with Mama. Daddy had already died, I didn't miss him at all. I loved Mama very much—but probably I shouldn't have stayed. I should have gone out on my own. If I had gone out on my own, I would have met somebody nice and married them. But look what happened, I stayed with Mama, and then when Mama died I went crazy out of my mind and I married Genevieve Snyder."

"Daddy, if you *hadn't* married Genevieve, I wouldn't be sitting here talking to you."

"You sure?"

"Of course. What do you think? I'm Mama's girl. I'm not anybody else's daughter."

"Then I suppose it was all for the good," sighed James Caskey. "Though it didn't seem much like it at the time."

"Daddy, you'll be fine. Everybody in Perdido knows I'm up here at Vanderbilt, and everybody in town's gone want to take care of you. Loneliness isn't gone be *your* problem. Well, for instance, just look at the number of Caskeys there are now! You know, when I was little, I was all by myself, I didn't have anybody to play with, I didn't have anybody to talk to. But good Lord, look what it's like now! Elinor came to town during the flood, and now there's Miriam and Frances, and Queenie showed up, and Queenie's got three children—"

"Don't forget Carl!"

"Wish I could! Anyway, Daddy, the town is full of family now. They snuck up on us. You will hardly notice I'm gone."

But a day or two following, while James Caskey was unwrapping the figurines, and ornaments, and plates he had purchased in Nashville, in his daughter's company and with his daughter's advice, it seemed as if each were a stone he was tossing down a deep, dry, black well that had opened itself wide at his feet.

Queenie Strickland worried that her children were too much exposed to their father's contaminating presence and conversation. She tried to keep them out of the house and removed from their father's baleful influence. She feared, however, that Malcolm was already lost. Carl had taken his elder son fishing on the upper Perdido, presented him with a gun on the first day of hunting season, had even allowed Malcolm to go with him to the racetrack in Cantonement one Saturday afternoon. Malcolm was easily won over to his father's camp by these masculine blandishments. One day, in anger that his mother had denied him a trifling privilege, Malcolm declared that he loved Carl very very much, and that he hated Queenie's guts.

Carl tended to ignore his daughter, believing a little girl beneath his notice. He thought if Queenie taught Lucille to sew and cook and flirt, she would turn out well enough.

With Malcolm all but lost, and Lucille in little danger, it was of greatest importance for Queenie to keep her younger son free of his father's influence. As she explained to James Caskey, "That boy is not like Malcolm, and he's certainly not like his daddy. He's so quiet and shy! He doesn't like the way his daddy talks. He doesn't like the way his daddy acts. I wish...I just *wish* he didn't have to live in the same house with Carl."

"Well," replied James, as he sat down in a chair on the other side of Queenie's desk in the outer office, "I don't know that it's so much worse for Danjo than it is for you and Lucille."

"It *is*. I'm used to it. I don't like it, but I'm used to it. Carl doesn't bother Lucille so much, 'cause she's a girl. He won't take Lucille out with him, see. He won't take her hunting, he won't take her with him to the track. That's the difference. And Carl keeps on talking about getting a gun for Danjo. A *gun*, James! And that child is only five years old!"

The telephone rang, and the conversation was broken off, not to be resumed that day. The next morning, James was at work early. As soon as Queenie arrived, and before she had even arranged her desk, James tapped on the glass and signaled for her to come into his office.

"Morning, James."

"Morning, Queenie. How'd you sleep?"

"Nightmares."

"Me too. I always have nightmares in an empty house."

"Oh, I know you miss your little girl! Have you heard from her?"

"I have. She has sent me three letters, and I get a postcard near about every day. I've got an album to put 'em in, went out and bought it last week."

"So Grace is doing all right up at Vanderbilt?"

"She is making one friend after another. She says she is so happy up there she can hardly stand it. She says she wants me to write her some bad news so she can come down off cloud nine."

"James, did you have something to say to me?" said Queenie, having noted from the first a distraction in her brother-in-law's manner.

"I did. Sit down, Queenie. I've been thinking about what you said yesterday."

"About what?"

"About Danjo."

Queenie nodded.

"Things didn't get any better last night, did they?"

She stopped and considered the matter a moment. "I hate to say it, James, but I think I am getting sort of used to Carl's being back. I mean, he doesn't go out beating people up anymore. I don't think he's stealing. As long as he's in one room at night and I'm in another that's all right—or at least it would be if it weren't for Danjo."

"That's what I wanted to talk to you about. I was thinking maybe you should get rid of Danjo."

"He's my preciousest!"

"I know, but, Queenie, you don't want him contaminated! That's the word you used yesterday."

"I sure don't, but what am I supposed to do with him?"

"Give him to me."

"To you? You don't want him!"

"How you know that! I do want him!"

"He's so little! What would you do with a five-year-old, James?"

"I'd raise him up right. I've had experience. I raised Grace, and as you know, most of that time I was working pretty much on my own. Genevieve was mostly with you in Nashville."

"Well, I know all that. What I mean is, what about all your pretty things?"

"I don't mind. Danjo is careful. He's been in my house before. And if some things get broken, that's all right. I can buy others. I'm not poor. I can build high shelves. Danjo will be just fine. So why don't you go on and give him to me? Queenie, I'm so lonesome without Grace, I cain't hardly stand it. I was moping around last night, just thinking that what I could use most in the world was a little boy to keep me company."

"And you think Danjo will do?"

"Danjo would be the best, Queenie!"

"I'd hate to give him up."

"Queenie, it's not like I'd be taking him to a different town—you could come see him all the time. And look at it this way: I wouldn't be taking him away from you, I'd just be taking him away from Carl."

"I'd like that," Queenie admitted. "Carl will raise holy hell."

"What's he gone do about it?"

"Come and take Danjo back, that's what."

"I'll shoot him," James promised complacently.

Queenie beat her heel rapidly on the floor. "Let me think about it, James." She got up and returned to her own office. In five minutes she was back.

"Well?" asked James.

"I don't want to give him up, I really don't. But it just seems so selfish of me, when I've got three and you've just lost the only one you ever had."

"That's right, Queenie. It would be real selfish of you to keep Danjo all to yourself. So why don't you go on and give him to me?"

"All right. *If* we can get him away from Carl."

"*I*'ll speak to Carl."

"You gone offer him money?"

"I don't know. Maybe. How much you think he'd sell Danjo for? A hundred dollars a month?"

Queenie considered. "What about a new car?"

Queenie was right. In exchange for a new automobile—Carl's choice and costing twelve hundred dollars—Danjo was given over to James Caskey for safekeeping. Ostensibly, the exchange was temporary, but no one was deceived. The boy was not consulted, but Danjo was so meek a child that he would doubtless have acquiesced to any proposition. Danjo was put in the old nursery in James's house, which had been freshly wallpapered and given a set of furniture. The boy was bewildered to think that he wouldn't have to share it with anyone. He cried a little when he left his mother, but he stopped his tears when she assured him that she would see him all the time. He had thought that he was being taken away from her forever, and even at that he had ventured no vehement protest.

The first weekend that Danjo spent in his new

home, he would not venture out of his room, and when James would peep in, his nephew would always be sitting very still on the edge of his bed. The boy appeared so constrained and unhappy that James forewent his usual reluctance to intrude, and finally ventured into the room. Leaning against a chifforobe just inside the door, he peered down at Danjo and said, "Am I gone have to send you back to your mama and daddy, Danjo?"

Danjo looked up, his eyes full of tears.

"I want you to stay, Danjo, but you're just not happy here, I guess."

"I am!"

James Caskey was puzzled. "You don't want to go home to your mama and daddy?"

Danjo considered this. "I miss Mama..." he ventured.

"But not your daddy?"

Danjo shook his head vigorously.

"Then why aren't you happier here with me? Why don't you run around and play? You used to play all the time. Do you miss Lucille and Malcolm?"

Danjo shook his head cautiously. "I don't want to break anything," he said in a low voice.

"Break anything? Break what?"

"Break your stuff."

James stared at the boy. "You mean you're not leaving this room 'cause you're afraid you're gone knock something over?"

Danjo nodded, and appeared very near tears again.

"Lord, Lord," cried James Caskey. "Don't you worry about that, Danjo! *I* don't care if you break something. How much stuff you suppose my girl Grace broke while she was growing up? How much stuff you guess Roxie breaks while she's cleaning this house? You think I can walk through a room without something falling to the floor and smashing? I cain't! And I don't expect you can, either. Danjo, I want you to be happy here. You know how much I've

39

got in this house. You breaking something's not gone make one little bit of difference. I've got closets full of junk, and I'm gone be going out buying more anyway. Now, I don't want you to run out of here and start pitching things against the wall—"

Danjo's eyes widened in horror at the suggestion.

"—but I do want you to enjoy yourself here. I want you at your ease."

"You do?"

"I sure do. Danjo, do you know what I paid for you?"

"You bought Daddy a car?"

"I did. It cost me one thousand two hundred dollars. I've made a big investment in you, Danjo. And you got to help pay it back."

"How?"

"By having a good time. By letting me watch you enjoy yourself here. By keeping me company, and making me not feel so sorry for myself because my little girl's gone away. Will you do that?"

"I'll try!" cried Danjo, and he ran across the room and hugged his uncle.

Perdido claimed that it had never seen a family to match the Caskeys when it came to giving children up and taking children in, switching offspring around as if they had been extra turkey platters or other household items that there might be an excess of in one house and a lack of in the next. Carl Strickland made no secret of the terms of the deal by which James Caskey got custody of his Danjo. That was a sale that had all the force of a deeded exchange of land in the eyes of Perdido. Thenceforth, Danjo belonged to James Caskey, and Perdido thought it was wonderful of James that he allowed the boy's mother to visit her son whenever she liked.

It seemed a perfect situation. Carl Strickland had his new automobile. Queenie Strickland was assured of her boy's moral and financial future. James Caskey had a child to take the place of the one who had grown up and gone away. And no one was happier with the situation than Danjo himself.

Rather than taking it as an affront that he had been sold off for the price of a new automobile, Danjo was comforted by the binding aspects of that transaction. He was less likely to be snatched away and carried back across town to the house in which he was assaulted, in varying degrees and in varying ways, by his brother, his sister, and his father, and where his mother had been his sole but inadequate comfort. He loved James Caskey. He never got over a sense of privilege of having a room all to himself, of living in a house that was quiet and filled with beautiful things, of being kissed and hugged rather than pinched and punched. The boy's only agony, and he kept it a deep secret, was the fear that someday his uncle would trade him off in turn, in exchange for a diamond ring, perhaps, or a little girl. Where would Danjo end up *then?*

Ten years before, the Caskeys had appeared a barren family to the rest of Perdido. There had been only James's little daughter Grace, a pale, whining thing hardly worth the attention her effeminate father paid her. Later Elinor and Queenie produced five children between them and divided them among the wanting Caskey households. It was as if Mary-Love and James had looked up and cried, *Good Lord, Elinor! For goodness' sake, Queenie! Y'all have got so many, and we don't have any, why don't y'all pass a couple of those children around so we can all enjoy them.* It wasn't quite like that, of course, not in the Caskey family, where a favor done was no more to be tolerated than a slap in the face—but the children were distributed nonetheless, so that each household had at least one. In consequence, the very texture of the entire family was altered, and despite individual animosities, the Caskeys seemed a younger, more vigorous and happier clan.

CHAPTER 31

Displacements

The stock market crashed on October 29, 1929, but no one in Perdido realized what effect that distant event—that strange crisis of faith and paper—would bring to bear upon each of them. The Caskeys, who perhaps might have had at least a crinkled brow or two of worry for what it would all mean to family and to the town, were occupied at that time with a more immediate matter: the day the stock market crashed, Carl Strickland attempted to murder Queenie.

Unpremeditated assaults rarely occur in the morning. Violent passions are most often engendered by accumulated heat, by alcohol, by weariness of the body—elements whose effects are generally felt most strongly in the evening or late at night. But Queenie Strickland raised her husband's ire at the breakfast table by refusing to give him fifteen dollars to visit the track. His unpredictably savage reaction only showed Perdido how close to the edge the man had always been, even when he appeared to live quite peaceably in their midst.

"Queenie, you've got the money!" he shouted across the kitchen table.

"Course I got it, but I'm gone spend it on food! How much you suppose I make?"

"I suppose you make plenty, that old man pays you plenty!"

"He doesn't! I make enough to feed this family, and that's all! Do you see me in new dresses? Where are Malcolm's new shoes? Is Lucille taking piano lessons? Do you hear a piano every afternoon when you come back from the track? If you need money so bad, why don't you go get yourself a job?"

"Give me the money, Queenie. You got it!"

"No," said Queenie. She got up from the table and motioned for Lucille and Malcolm to leave the room. They did so, making faces at their father's back. With relief, a moment later, Queenie heard the front door slam as the children went out.

"The money's mine," said Carl, getting up from the table and pushing it away from him so that all the dishes rattled, and a cup rolled off and smashed on the linoleum. "Everything you got is mine. Where is it?"

"Carl, get away from me!"

He pushed her against the sink. He grabbed handfuls of flesh around her thick waist and squeezed until she cried out in pain. She attempted to pull away. He pressed her harder. He momentarily let go, and with his right hand ripped the pocket from the front of her dress. Nothing fell out but the two coins kept in reserve for his dead eyes.

Seeing them, Carl retreated. Queenie gasped for breath, and stared at her husband. He seemed to her suddenly crazed, as if he had lost both reason and control in a single stroke. He turned wildly, lifted the table by a corner, and toppled it onto its side. All the dishes smashed, and Queenie's legs were splattered and burned with hot coffee. She cried out and staggered toward the back door.

Carl ran up behind her, doubled up his fist and hit her as hard as he could in the kidney. Queenie's breath forsook her, and she fell face down in the pile of broken crockery. As she rolled over in an attempt to rise, Carl kicked her three times in the belly— short, sharp, powerful kicks. Queenie stretched out in a long moan.

Carl placed his booted foot on her head, pressed down and ground Queenie's face into the broken fragments of a white porcelain cup. The yellow linoleum grew bloody beneath Queenie's prostrate body.

As the pressure of the boot was withdrawn, Queenie struggled to raise her head. One eye was masked with blood. Malcolm and Lucille stood horror-struck outside the kitchen door, peering through the screen. Lucille shrieked and ran away. Malcolm followed her a moment after.

Carl picked up a chair and smashed it across his wife's back.

Lucille's shrieks brought Florida Benquith to her kitchen window next door. Seeing the fleeing Malcolm, she went outside and hurried over to the Stricklands' house. She peered in at the back door, and saw Carl Strickland, like an overfed demon, sitting on his wife's rear end, and shredding open the back of her dress with a vegetable peeler held convulsively in both hands.

"Queenie! Queenie!" Florida screamed.

Blood welled up out of the long stripes in Queenie's back, where the potato peeler had cut through the material and flayed open her skin.

Florida ran back to her house and, not taking the time to say a word to her astonished husband, took up his loaded shotgun from its place in the corner of the dining room, and flung herself out the door once

45

more. When she was still twenty feet from the house, and long before she could actually see through the Stricklands' back door, she fired the gun once, blowing a hole in the screen.

"Carl Strickland, I'm gone shoot you!" she hollered as she ran up to the door and into the house.

Startled by the blast of the shotgun, Carl rose from his wife's back, and fled through the house, out the front door, and across the front yard. Florida left Queenie in a pool of blood on the kitchen floor and followed him. As she got out onto the front porch, Carl was just flinging himself into his automobile. Florida fired again, and knocked out a side window of the car. Carl got the engine started and he barreled off.

Florida Benquith dropped the shotgun on the grass and looked all around her, astonished. Miz Daughtry across the street stood on her front steps in her nightdress. The Moye children perched open-mouthed at the end of their sidewalk.

"Call Elinor Caskey!" Florida shouted at Miz Daughtry, and ran back inside. Dr. Benquith was already there, and said only, "She's still alive..."

No one had any idea where Carl Strickland had gone. Oscar went to the sheriff and remarked coldly, "If Carl does come back, Mr. Key, and you happen to see him, let us know, will you, so that we can get Queenie out of his way. This next time, Queenie might not be so lucky."

Embarrassed, Charley Key asked, "How is Miz Strickland, Oscar?"

"Three broken ribs, dislocated jaw. Lost most of the vision in her right eye. Other than that, just cut up and bruised."

"Well," said the sheriff, "I'm sorry to hear it. I notified the state police. Over in Florida, too. Told 'em Mr. Strickland hung out a lot down at Cantonement. They're looking for him there."

46

"I don't care where he is, as long as he's not in Perdido."

"I'm gone make sure he don't hurt nobody else," Charley said staunchly.

"You could have stopped *this* from happening," Oscar pointed out, and walked out of the office.

Queenie spent ten days at Sacred Heart Hospital in Pensacola. During that time, Malcolm and Lucille stayed with Elinor, and were given the guest bedroom at the front of the house—a room so little used that it hadn't even been given a name, though later it would be called, "the children's room." Elinor and Oscar had anticipated some difficulty with Malcolm and Lucille, who were not known as model children, but the brother and sister appeared subdued and genuinely concerned for their mother's well-being. Every day Bray drove either Elinor or Mary-Love or James down to visit Queenie, and every day one or another of her children would go along. Queenie's attitude during her recuperation was one almost of relief: "If this is what I had to go through to get rid of Carl for once and all, then I am happy to have done it. I'm just gone have to hope he doesn't try to come back for more."

Queenie was brought back to Perdido on the eighth of November, and installed in Elinor's house. Until Carl was found, it was not thought safe for her to stay in her own home. He had caught her there by surprise twice before, and might possibly do so again. While she recuperated at Elinor's, Queenie was given Frances's room, because it had its own bath.

When she returned home from school that day, Frances ran into the house, up the stairs, and into her own bedroom. She wanted to hug Queenie, but Queenie cried, "Lord, no, child! You cain't touch me, look at my face! You ought to see my arms and back under these bedclothes! I am a sight for men and

47

angels! You squeeze my hand, though," she said, holding out her fingers for the timid child to grasp.

"Queenie, I'm real glad you're back from the hospital," said Frances.

"No, you're not," said Queenie.

"What do you mean by that?" asked Elinor, peering into the room through the window that opened onto the porch.

"Hey, Mama," said Frances. "I *am* glad she's back."

"No, you're not," said Queenie, " 'cause I took over your room."

"Oh, that's all right," said Frances. " 'Cause you're sick, and I'm not."

"I'm not sick, I'm just so sore all over I cain't hardly move without wanting to sit down and write out my will, that's all."

Frances left Queenie alone and joined her mother on the porch. "Mama," she asked, "if Queenie's in here, then where am I gone sleep?"

"I'm putting you in the front room, darling," replied Elinor.

Frances was dumbstruck. Her fear of the front room and the undersized closet door to the right of the hearth was as strong as ever. She still would not remain in the house alone, even during brightest day; she still listened every night from her bed for the sound of that closet door in the next room being surreptitiously opened, and of whatever was inside emerging cautiously into the dark.

Crushed by the terror that her mother's simple revelation inspired in her, Frances was unable to speak another word. She wandered off in a daze. In her worst fears, Frances had never imagined that she would ever actually have to spend a *night* in that front room. The thought was too horrible to imagine—that she would be forced to lie in that bed alone, at night, and stare straight across at the weird little door, waiting for whatever was inside slowly to turn the knob and squeeze out. It would not matter that

Queenie would be in the next room, through the passage where the linens were stored; that Lucille and Malcolm and her parents were across the hall, that Zaddie was downstairs. The entire town of Perdido might squeeze into the house and arrange themselves along the walls, but it would make no difference if Frances had to sleep alone in the front room. She thought she would surely die.

Now she found herself standing before the door of that very room, not having realized where her distracted footsteps were taking her. She softly turned the knob and peered in. As always, the room was dim and cool. No air moved in it. It smelled old— older than a room in any house in Perdido could possibly be. To Frances it smelled as if whole generations of Caskeys had died there in that room— as if decade after decade, Caskey mothers had been delivered of stillborn infants in that bed; as if an uninterrupted line of Caskey husbands had murdered their adulterous wives and stuck them in that chifforobe; as if a hundred skeletons with rotting flesh and tatters of clothing were heaped in that little closet, jostled in among the fur and feathers. For the first time in her memory, Frances noticed that the clock on the mantel had been wound and was ticking. She was about to shut the door when the clock chiming the quarter-hour seemed to beckon her. Frances resisted its call, anxiously pulled the door shut, and fled down the hall, not daring to look behind her. She ran back onto the porch and buried her head in her mother's lap.

"Darling, what's wrong?" said Elinor.

"I don't want to sleep in the front room!" cried Frances.

"Why not?"

"I'm scared."

"Scared of what?"

Frances paused, and wondered how to frame her reply. "I'm scared of that closet."

"That closet?" Elinor laughed. "There's nothing in that closet. Just my clothes and my shoes and my hats. You've seen inside that closet."

"Let me sleep in the room Lucille and Malcolm are in. They can sleep in the front room."

"They've already settled in, and they're doing fine where they are. I'm not going to move them."

"Then let Queenie sleep in there! Let me have my own room back, Mama!"

"Queenie needs to have a bathroom of her own. And I want her to be near me, darling, so I can hear her if she calls."

"Let me go over to James's, then."

"James has his hands full with Danjo." Elinor's voice wasn't as soft now as when Frances had made her first plea. "Do you have any other suggestions?"

"I'll even go stay with Grandmama."

"Miss Mary-Love would never let me hear the end of it, if I sent you over there when I have got an empty bed in this house. I don't want to hear another word. You're going to sleep in the front room until Queenie is well enough to go home and until we're sure that Carl is not going to bother her anymore. Do you understand?"

"Elinor!" Queenie called through the window.

Elinor stepped over to the window and peered in. "Queenie, can I do something for you?"

"You sure can. I couldn't help hearing all of that and I want you to put me in the front room, and let Frances have her room back."

"Queenie, I hope you weren't taking Frances's nonsense seriously."

"She doesn't want me in her bed, and I can understand that. She wants her own little room back. If this were my room, I wouldn't want to give it up either."

"Queenie, I'm not letting you move. Now you listen, you need your own bathroom, and I want you where I can sit out here on the porch and talk to you through the window. That's why you are where you are, and there is no reason on this earth why Frances can't sleep in the front room. It is only six feet away. The front room is not at the end of the earth."

Frances listened to this conversation with trembling.

"Frances," said her mother sternly, "come with me."

Frances followed her mother down the hall into the front room. Elinor unhesitatingly went over to the closet and pulled open the door. "Now do you see that there is nothing inside this closet? I have got so much stuff in there that there is not *room* for anything to be hiding in there."

The child made no reply, but only hung her head.

"Frances, have you been talking to Ivey Sapp? Has Ivey been telling you stories about things that are supposed to eat up little girls?"

"No, ma'am!"

"Are you sure?"

"Yes, ma'am."

"Well, if Ivey does start to try and fill your head with nonsense like that, I don't want you to listen to her. Ivey doesn't always know what she's talking about. Ivey gets things wrong."

"Then there *are* things that eat you?"

"Not in this closet," replied her mother with a disquieting evasiveness.

"Where are they then?"

"Nothing's going to eat *you,* darling," said Elinor as she closed the closet door and seated herself on the edge of the bed. "Come here, Frances." Frances went over timidly to her mother and Elinor lifted her up beside her.

"Yes, ma'am?"

"Now, we go out together sometimes on the river in Bray's little boat, right?"

"Yes, ma'am."

"Are you afraid then?"

51

"No, ma'am."

"Why not? Other little girls would be afraid. Lucille Strickland won't go out in a boat on the Perdido."

"It's 'cause you're there, Mama, that's why I'm not afraid."

Elinor hugged Frances close, and said, "That's right, you're my little girl, and nothing's ever going to happen to you. Besides, *you* of all people never have to be afraid of that river. So why are you afraid to stay in this room, when you know I'm right across the hall?"

"I don't know," said Frances, troubled. " 'Cause it might get me before you could come in and save me."

"What is 'it'?"

"I don't know."

"Then how do you know it's there?"

"I can feel it, Mama!"

Elinor pried her daughter's arms from around her waist, pushed her aside, and looked directly in her face. "Now, listen to me, Frances," she said in a patient but determined voice, "there is nothing in this room to hurt you, you understand? If you see anything, it's only your imagination. It's shadows, it's dust catching the light. If you hear anything, it's only your imagination. It's the house settling on its foundations, or it's the furniture creaking. If you feel anything touching you, it's your nerves going to sleep or it's a mosquito landing on your arm. That's all it is. You're dreaming. You're dreaming that you hear something, you're dreaming that you see something, you're dreaming that something is trying to pull you out of bed. Do you understand? Nothing will happen to you in this room because I won't let it."

Her mother showed her that some of her clothes had already been brought in and hung up in the chifforobe. Elinor pulled out drawers and made her daughter admit how sweet the sachet inside smelled. She opened the curtains and showed Frances that the view of the levee and Miss Mary-Love's house was very nearly the same from here as from her own room. At the last, Elinor turned the key in the lock of the door of the small closet, and said, "Look, Frances, I'm locking the door. So you don't have to worry. If there's anything inside there, it won't be able to get out now. You'll be perfectly safe. And just remember, if you hear anything or see anything or feel anything, don't pay any attention. It's just your imagination. You're *my* little girl, and nothing can happen to you."

CHAPTER 32

Locked or Unlocked

That first night of Queenie's return to Perdido, Frances played out her entire repertoire of procrastination tricks, but ingenious as she was, at last she was roused out of her father's lap on the porch and told that she must absolutely go to bed.

"Why are you being like this?" her father asked.

"She's afraid to go to bed," Elinor explained.

"You have slept by yourself since you were a *little* girl," cried Oscar in surprise.

"She's not afraid of being by herself," Elinor continued, "she's afraid of the front room."

"What's in the front room?" Oscar asked. "I can hardly remember the last time I was even in there. I remember looking at the new curtains, but that was years and years ago! Elinor, have you taken in a boarder that I don't know anything about?"

But Frances didn't laugh and clung to her father more tightly still.

"Elinor," said Oscar, seeing that his daughter

really was frightened, "cain't we let her sleep with us?"

"No," said Elinor. "Then she'd want to sleep with us forever."

"I wouldn't!" protested Frances. "Just tonight!"

"Then tomorrow night, then the night after that."

"Your mama," said Oscar, "wants you in the front room, so I guess I'm just gone have to carry you up there."

Oscar did so, and laid her in the bed beneath the covers. He waggled the curtains to show her that no one was hiding behind them, ostentatiously knelt down on the floor and peered under the bed, opened the door of the passage that led to Frances's own room where Queenie was already asleep, and rattled the knob of the closet to show that it remained locked. He kissed Frances good-night and left the room. Snaking his hand back through the door, he pushed the button that turned out the overhead light.

After her father had shut the door, Frances could no longer assure herself that the front room was connected with the rest of the house. She was cut off from her parents' protection; they would never hear her if she called. The front room was real enough but those doors no longer communicated with the house in which Elinor and Oscar Caskey lived. Those windows no longer looked out on the same familiar scene. Frances trembled now to think what unimaginable space might lie behind those doors, what unexpected somber landscape might be imperfectly discerned through those windows. She lay rigidly in the bed, staring into the unsettling blackness, listening in a terrified stupor for something to begin shifting about inside the closet. Gradually her eyes became accustomed to the dark, and she faintly made out the room's objects as inky shadows against more blackness. The cast-iron chandelier above the foot of her bed was her point of reference. She stared at it with concentration. It seemed to sway but there was

56

no air moving in the room. Frances balled herself up and burrowed beneath the covers. Her stifled breath was hot and wet under the starched sheets.

Occasionally she heard creaks. Once she was startled by what sounded to her like a marble dropping to the floor and rolling a short distance.

Eventually she fell asleep. She must have, for Zaddie awakened her in the morning, pulling back the curtains on a dim overcast day. Frances felt the relief a man feels when he has narrowly escaped a terrible death, as when a pursuing animal is momentarily distracted and turns aside, forgetting his quarry.

"Y'all having breakfast out on the porch this morning, Frances," said Zaddie, kneeling at the side of the bed, and slipping on the child's socks for her.

"Zaddie, I'm hungry! Can I have three pieces of toast today?"

"You sure can! I tell you what, if you'll finish up your dressing, I'll go downstairs right this minute and put that bread in the oven."

"I can dress myself," said Frances. "You don't have to help me."

"I like to! You're my little girl!"

Frances hugged Zaddie. "Zaddie," she whispered, "I'm so glad you didn't go away to that college for colored people."

"Well, if I'd done that, who'd take care of my little girl? Sure not nobody in town loves you like I love you!" Zaddie laughed, and left Frances alone once again.

Frances made a little show of her morning bravery, witnessed only by herself. With no apparent hesitation she pulled open the door of the chifforobe and placed her folded nightclothes in the darkest corner of the bottom shelf. She went alone into the connecting passage, actually shutting herself in, and took her time in selecting a fresh towel. Returning to the room, she dropped a pin so that she could lean down and peer, as if inadvertently, under the bed.

Perhaps, after all, the danger in the room had been no more than her imagination. Perhaps, after all, there was nothing to fear. Zaddie called her from the hallway. "Frances, toast's ready!"

Frances grinned to herself and looked around the room. As she was about to leave, glowing in her confidence, she decided to try to rid herself of her last piece of fear. She'd rattle the knob of the locked closet door.

"Coming!" she called to Zaddie, and thinking only of the food she was about to eat, she ran across the room and turned the knob of the closet door, waiting for that comforting rattle that would show her that whatever was inside—and there wasn't anything anyway—still couldn't get out at her.

But the knob did not rattle. Instead it turned smoothly in her grasp, and the door swung open to reveal the vista of crowded fur and feathers, showing Frances that the danger all night long had been inestimably greater than she had imagined.

Somehow, during the night, the closet door had been unlocked.

Frances ran to her mother, and told Elinor—with all the firmness that she could muster—that she was never going to sleep in the front room again.

"Hush!" said Elinor. "Are you still going on about that room?"

Frances nodded dolefully.

"Did anything happen last night?"

"No," replied Frances in a hot whisper, kneeling on the swing and burying her face against her mother's neck. "But this morning when I got up the closet door was unlocked."

Elinor made no response to this.

Defensively, Frances cried: "You locked it yesterday afternoon, Mama! I saw you! Daddy jiggled the knob last night and it was still locked! And when I got up this morning, it was *un*locked. Please let me sleep with you and Daddy tonight."

58

Elinor took her daughter to the front room, pulled on the handle of the closet door, and demonstrated that it was indeed still locked.

"Who locked it?" cried Frances, staring at the door in another agony of terror.

"No one!" cried Elinor. "It was never unlocked. You dreamed it, darling."

"I didn't!"

"You are worrying Oscar and me to death with this business, Frances. I don't want to hear it mentioned again. I want you to get it through your head that you are going to stay in this room until Queenie is well enough to go home, do you understand?"

"Yes, ma'am," replied Frances despairingly.

That night, Frances was summarily put between the covers, hastily kissed, and promptly abandoned to the darkness of the room and the infidel closet.

For the several weeks of Queenie's convalescence, Frances nightly went through her agony in the front room. One night her terror would perhaps be a bit less, and she would think, *I'm getting used to it. Nothing's ever happened.* The next night, however, her fear would be greater, and she would think, *It's just waiting until I'm completely off my guard.* Elinor did not repeat the experiment of trying the lock, but would merely say, "It's nonsense, Frances, complete nonsense. You know there's nothing in that closet anyway except my clothes and hats and shoes." During the day the door was always locked. It was only at night that the closet began to play its tricks. Then the door was sometimes locked, sometimes not. Every night, after Frances had lain in bed for a time without even thinking of trying to fall asleep, she would quietly rise and walk over and try the knob. No matter which way she anticipated, *locked* or *unlocked,* she was always wrong. As time passed, she began to make a game of it, and would stand before the door and make a prediction as to whether the knob were locked or unlocked—whether it would turn cleanly, or jar in her hand. She always chose wrong.

She became accustomed even to this maddening pattern, and her bravery in attempting the door always seemed in her mind to defuse the real danger of the closet. After thus proving herself, she was allowed to sleep undisturbed for the remainder of the night.

One night, however, she awakened suddenly, borne up out of sleep with the presentiment that something was very wrong. The room was very dark, and the house was quiet and still. She somehow knew that everyone in the house was asleep but her. Without thinking, she rose in the bed, kicked the pillows aside, and pulled open the drapes over the front window. The room became less dark. Frances now could see the black outline of the closet door. She could see the brass knob, gleaming a faint gold. She had locked the closet door herself. She was certain no one had come into the room to undo that brave piece of work. If she tried the knob now, however, would the door be locked?

She would pull on the knob. If the door remained locked, then she'd be safe and could go back to sleep; if it were unlocked, then whatever was inside would jump out and kill her.

Frances prayed her usual ineffectual prayer and started to climb down from the bed.

A rectangle of light, white-blue and cold, suddenly gleamed around the closet door. It was bright enough to show the colors of the carpet fringe. The left-hand side of the rectangle of light began to grow wider; the other three sides remained the same narrow strips. After a moment of observing this merely as a phenomenon of geometrical progression, Frances realized that it was the result of the door of the closet slowly opening.

* * *

The hallway down the center of the second floor of the Caskey home was wide, with a long runner of dark blue carpet over the parquet floors. At one end was the door with stained glass leading to the narrow unscreened porch at the front of the house. At the other end was the landing and a great window, halfway between the first and second floors, looking out over the back yard and the levee. Frances fled down this corridor, desperate to cry out. The doors of all the other bedrooms were shut. She could scarcely believe that her parents were actually behind one of them, Queenie behind another, Lucille and Malcolm sleeping peacefully behind the third. She took hold of the banister knob at the top of the stairs and turned and looked back down the hallway. A whiteness, not like sunlight or lamplight or moonlight, now formed a rectangle—very like the first one around the closet door—around the front room door that she had pulled shut behind her. To be as bright as it was, the room must have been filled with the unnatural bluish-white illumination. Frances was certain that the closet door was opened full. Whatever had been inside the closet now completely possessed the front room. Perhaps it was looking under the bed for her, just as she had always checked under the bed for it. As Frances stared, transfixed, waiting for that door to open as the other one had only moments before, the refulgence began to seep out into the hallway like mist. By its light she could now make out the pattern of the wallpaper; she could see the lines in the parquet along the walls.

Frances dared not disturb her parents. She felt certain that the minute they stepped into the hallway the glow would somehow dissipate and she would be returned to the front room, chastised for her cries and her fear. She decided, therefore, to go downstairs to Zaddie, who slept in a small room off the kitchen. Zaddie would give her a blanket, and Frances would roll up in it on the floor and be perfectly content. The light from the closet could do as it pleased.

It did not occur to Frances that whatever was in the front room might mean danger to anyone but herself. Whatever was in the closet, whatever caused the door to lock and unlock, whatever produced this misty light and now wandered about the front room, was interested in Frances alone.

She ran down the stairs and paused on the landing. Behind the great window the night was still black. The water oaks were only massive amorphous shadows. She couldn't see the levee. She turned once more to look back. The front room door had been thrown wide open, and the light poured out into the corridor, bleaching the colors there. The panes of colored glass in the porch door reflected the light in sickly hues.

Frances closed her eyes and convulsively grasped the banister, momentarily frozen to the spot, when with the sound of a great explosion, the staircase window behind her shattered. Thousands of shards of glass and splinters of wood showered down upon her, and Frances no longer held back her screams.

CHAPTER 33

The Croker Sack

Elinor and Oscar were wakened immediately by the noise of the explosion and the screams of both Frances and Queenie. As Elinor rose in her bed, there was the sound of a gunshot, and the window of their bedroom shattered and a picture on the opposite wall crashed to the floor. The house seemed to be under fire from the direction of the levee.

"For God's sake Elinor, get down!" cried Oscar.

Elinor paid no attention. She leaped from the bed and ran out of the room, calling "Frances! Frances!"

There were more shots. Elinor heard windows breaking on the first floor. There were dull thumps as the bullets struck the side of the house. A window seemed to break somewhere inside the house, and Elinor heard Zaddie's scream.

Queenie stood in the doorway of her room, holding herself up weakly by the doorjamb. She had her thumb on the switch to turn on the hall light.

"No!" cried Elinor. "Don't! They'll be able to see inside the house!"

"It must be Carl!" cried Queenie wildly.

A shot, aimed through the broken staircase window, whizzed down the corridor and smashed three panes of stained glass in the door at the opposite end.

"Mama?" said Malcolm tentatively. He and Lucille stood in the open doorway of the children's room, staring at the broken glass at their feet.

"Go back inside your room," said Elinor quickly. "Sit down on the floor and don't move."

The children hesitated.

"Now!"

Lucille and Malcolm retreated inside and slammed the door after them.

"Queenie, go back in and sit down in that chair in the corner. Don't get up no matter what."

"It's Carl," cried Queenie in desperation, "trying to kill us all!"

The shots, which had briefly stopped, resumed. Elinor stood upright against the doorway of her room. With resounding thumps, two bullets embedded themselves in the ceiling of the hallway.

"Frances!" she called.

"Mama?" The terrified voice came weakly from below.

"Where are you?"

"I'm on the stairs! I'm cut! The glass cut me!"

"Frances, don't turn on any lights. And don't try to come back upstairs."

"Miss El'nor!"

"Zaddie?"

"Yes, ma'am!" Zaddie called up.

"Zaddie, don't turn on any lights. Can you see Frances?"

"Yes, ma'am."

"Zaddie, come get me," whispered Frances.

"Walk up the stairs and get her," said Elinor, "then

carry her down to the front hallway. Don't go near any windows."

"You want me to call the police, Miss El'nor?"

"No," replied Elinor, "Oscar's calling them now."

Oscar reached out from behind and put his hand on Elinor's shoulder. "I cain't get Mr. Key on the line. Are we sure it's Carl?"

"Who else is going to be firing bullets into the house, Oscar?"

"Nobody else, I guess. Is everybody standing away from the windows, Elinor?" He whispered, as if by his voice, at such a distance, Carl Strickland would find them out.

"Lucille and Malcolm are in the children's room. They're safe—at least for now—because that's at the front of the house. Queenie's sitting in the corner chair in Frances's room. Some of the shots went through the screens, and that inside window is broken, but if Queenie sits still, she'll be all right."

"Where's Frances?"

"Downstairs with Zaddie. I told them to sit in the hallway. Frances got cut when the staircase window broke."

"Is she cut bad?"

"I don't know."

"Let me go call Dr. Benquith."

Oscar went back into the sitting room, which had no window open to the back of the house and the madman firing there, and telephoned Leo Benquith. He returned to the door, saying, "He's coming right over, but I told him to be careful, he should—"

Elinor was no longer there.

He called for her frantically.

"Hush!" she cried from the landing.

She was on her knees, inching her way across the glass-littered floor. Once past the danger of the exposed staircase window, Elinor got to her feet and descended the stairs. Broken glass crackled beneath her feet. "I'm going to see to Frances, Oscar! You

65

stay up there. Make sure Queenie and the children stay where they are!"

"Elinor, you shouldn't have left me!"

"Mama!" cried Frances. Regardless of the splinters and shards of glass, Elinor seated herself on the bottom step. She held out her arms to her daughter, and the child leaped into them.

"Frances, did anything get in your eyes? Can you see me?"

They heard more shots and the splintering of wood. "He's aiming for the lattice," said Zaddie quietly.

"Mama, I'm bleeding!"

"Yes, but can you still see all right? Out of both eyes."

"Yes, ma'am."

"All right, then," said Elinor, pushing her away with a kiss. "You hold on to Zaddie now, you hear? Don't let go of Zaddie. And Zaddie, you stay down low. Whoever it is is still on the levee, but he's broken every window in the back of the house and he may start to come around to one side or the other. If he does that, I want you and Frances to crawl into the pantry and shut the door, you hear?"

There was another shot, but this time from inside the house.

"Mama!"

"Shhh! That's your daddy, shooting out the window back at Carl. Trouble is, I don't think Daddy could hit anybody if he were standing right in front of him, holding up the barrel."

Elinor stood and moved quickly to the front door. As she put her hand on the knob Frances called out in an agony, "Mama, where are you going?"

"Shhh!" said Zaddie, grabbing Frances around the waist to prevent her from going after her mother. "Miss El'nor, you gone take care of things?"

"Zaddie," said Elinor, as she eased herself out the door, "I'm going to try."

The door closed behind Elinor, and Zaddie and

Frances were left hugging each other in the midst of debris, darkness, confusion, and fear.

Carl Strickland sat comfortably on the path atop the levee behind Oscar Caskey's house. He had two rifles, a double-barreled shotgun, a crate of .22 ammunition and a box of shotgun shells. He had been startled by a bluish-white light suffusing the upstairs hallways of the Caskey house, but by that same light he had been able to smash the large staircase window in the back. That light had immediately winked out, and it was a disappointment to Carl that no other had come on. The screams he had heard had satisfied him that he had at least frightened the household, even if he had not been so lucky as to kill anyone. Carl had been expecting the sheriff to drive up, but no one had come. He had not anticipated being so much at his leisure in this matter, and had begun wondering, since the inhabitants of the house appeared so passive in their defense, whether he ought not move down and around to the side of the house and fire into the windows there. He knew from his wife's distinctive scream which room Queenie was in. For good measure he had fired another shot through the second-floor screened porch and grinned when he heard more glass break in the interior. *That* was Queenie's room. He imagined the bullet burying itself in the folds of his wife's ample flesh.

He had seen the burst of fire from another window of the second floor, but the bullet came nowhere near him. *That* must be Oscar Caskey, Carl thought, and returned the fire with far greater accuracy.

If they're armed too, Carl considered, then maybe it was time to get out of here. He'd have other opportunities.

He fired two more shots at the house, emptying the loaded guns. Then shoving the weapons into a croker sack with the ammunition, he stood up, brushed himself off, and scuttled down the river side of the levee, using the heavy sack as a drag and a balance.

He heard a car in the distance. *That* is the police, he said to himself, and he heaved the sack into the boat in which he had crossed from the opposite bank. He pushed the boat farther into the water until it floated free, then climbed in himself, taking care to keep the craft steady.

Just as he was lifting the paddles, he was startled by a subdued splash upstream, but that might have been anything at all. He peered up into the darkness, but saw nothing. He paddled swiftly across the river, but all his energy couldn't prevent the current from propelling the boat at a sharp downstream angle. The northern shore of the Perdido, which was not banked by a levee, was soft and marshy. Beyond was a vast grove of ancient live oaks, and hidden among these was the automobile he had received from James Caskey in exchange for his younger son.

There was no moon, and the sky was overcast. The Perdido ran silently, smoothly, quickly, and relentlessly in the direction of the whirlpool at the junction a few hundred yards downstream.

Carefully, Carl climbed out of the boat. His foot sank deep into the soft mud of the riverbank, closing over the top of his left shoe. He drew it up with an expression of disgust, and advanced to firmer ground dragging the boat behind him. The live oaks in this grove were some of the largest trees in all of Alabama, and very likely the oldest. In an area of three or four acres several score of the trees, which retained their leathery leaves all winter, stood as black domes, their lower branches so massive that their extremities dragged the ground. Every tree thus formed a closed canopy, and underneath these living umbrellas festooned with Spanish moss, no grass would grow, no animals took shelter, and even a moonlit night was black. Children who had no fear or scruples about riding their bicycles over Indian burial mounds refused to play here. The trees and the grove were majestic, but unpleasantly so, as if they had been conceived as a monument to someone who had been here long before the Indians, the Spanish, the French, the English, and the Americans, all of whom had laid claim, in succession, to the grove.

Carl intended to hide the boat beneath one of these great canopies, for he could be reasonably confident that it would not be disturbed. He wasn't yet finished with the Caskeys or his wife.

He took out the croker sack and laid it carefully on the ground in a sort of clearing between two of the trees close to the bank of the river. Then he dragged the boat to the nearest of the live oaks, backed through the drooping curtain of branches and into the interior of the shrouded space. He could see nothing. He cried out softly when a strand of moss suddenly draped itself across his face. He unceremoniously dropped the boat near the vast trunk of the live oak and then, with groping arms outstretched before him, carefully retraced his steps. The wind sighed through the branches, and again a piece of moss fell across his face, as a net might be thrown over a creeping animal. When he reached up to brush it away, his fingers became entangled, and he tore the moss impatiently from its branch.

His exploring hands struck against a drooping branch that he had not seen. Once he emerged from the umbrella, the black night would seem light in comparison to this impenetrability.

He was pushing carefully ahead, hoping not to strike his head or become entangled in the smaller branches, when his step was arrested by a clatter outside the perimeter of the tree. He instantly knew it for the sound of his guns being tossed together. The sound of splitting wood, and another, more prolonged clatter told him that his crate of ammunition had been split open, its contents scattered.

"Hey!" he called, but his voice was neither as loud

nor as belligerent as he had intended. He pressed quickly through the curtain of branches, and again stood beneath the open sky.

In the clearing where he had left the croker sack stood a woman, dressed in a white nightdress that gleamed from the river water with which it was soaked. Her back was to Carl as she picked up one of the rifles and effortlessly tossed it into the river. Carl ran forward. The woman, without hurrying, picked up the other two guns and flung them into the water as well. She turned then and faced Carl.

It was Elinor Caskey.

"Queenie said it was you firing from the levee."

He rushed at her, with one hand raised to strike her. With an inconsequential motion of her own arm, she batted him away.

The force of the casual blow knocked him to the ground.

He stared up at her incredulously. He could scarcely make out the features of her face in the darkness, but the clinging nightdress continued to gleam.

"My guns..." Carl began hesitantly.

"I needed the croker sack," Elinor said.

He got quickly to his feet. He circled around her, unsure. Had she really hit him hard enough to knock him to the earth, or had he only lost his balance and fallen? He was behind her. "What for?" he asked.

In her fleeting profile as she turned, he caught a small smile.

"Oh," Elinor returned, "for you, Carl."

He punched her in the belly with all his strength. But it wasn't flesh there, it was something more giving and resilient. Elinor seemed to stand even straighter after the blow; she raised one arm. Something—not a hand—was clamped on Carl's shoulder.

With one sudden, sure application of pressure Carl was driven to the earth. Because it was applied to

70

only one shoulder, one side of Carl's body was instantly compressed. The clavicle gave way first, and then the ribs were jammed together and cracked. His lung was pierced with bone fragments and an artery was severed. The thigh bone was jammed up through the pelvis, the kneecap shattered against the ground. The shin and foot were crushed beneath the force.

Carl cried out, but the cry was strangled as his lung filled with blood.

One side of him remained whole but the other was squeezed into a third of its former space.

With a similar motion, Elinor brought the appendage that was not a hand down on Carl's other shoulder. She pressed it swiftly toward the earth.

Carl's face gaped up at her. His whole body was mangled, nearly all the bones dislocated, ligaments torn, organs displaced. The backbone remained intact, but it served only to curve him into the shape of a ball. He was half as tall as before. Instinctively he attempted to straighten himself, to stand up, but his body of course could not obey. Only his neck stretched upward a bit and his battered chin lifted into the night air.

Suddenly, Elinor dropped down before him, but the motion was not that of a woman squatting, or falling to her knees. It was the movement of some other sort of creature entirely. Carl heard Elinor's dress tear in a dozen places, as if it no longer fit the body that it encased. Her face was only a foot from his, and in the darkness he could see that her countenance had become wide and flat and round; the eyes bulged, and were huge; her mouth was monstrous, lipless, and it hissed wetly in a grin that had nothing human about it.

Her arms were once more lifted on either side of him. He gasped and winced against the blow that he was certain would kill him. But the blow did not come, only darkness, and the overpowering odor of burlap.

She was drawing the croker sack over his body.

Carl prayed for death, but death did not come. Neither did unconsciousness. Though his body below the neck seemed a continuing explosion of pain, his head maintained an unmerciful clarity through it all.

The pain, he considered, could not be worse, not in a thousand deaths, not in a thousand years of hell.

But Carl was wrong; the pain did become worse, for he was suddenly jerked up into the air inside the croker sack, and carried along upside down. The sack didn't drag the earth, or strike against Elinor's knees, so she must have been carrying him in one hand, and at arm's length. But what woman—what *man*—was as strong as that? Carl's brain filled with blood. His broken limbs dropped down around his head inside the croker sack until he was stifled with them. The fragments of his left arm were smothering him. Carl Strickland had been a big man, and now he was being carried along in a sack that wouldn't have properly held his own daughter.

The confusion of broken limbs that pressed against his face didn't smother him quickly enough, for his consciousness lasted long enough for him to realize that he was being carefully carried into the river. Elinor waded slowly into the water. At the top of his head, he perceived the river water permeating the burlap. Then more strongly, pressing the fabric against his ear, he felt the current of the river. Its ever stronger odor invaded the close confines of the sack, and he tasted the mud of the Perdido as water began to fill the bag and pour into his mouth.

It wasn't the torn arteries, the punctured lungs, the ruptured organs, or the shattered bones that killed Queenie's husband. Carl Strickland drowned in Perdido water.

CHAPTER 34

The Caskey Conscience

On the night that Carl Strickland fired wantonly into Oscar Caskey's house, the sheriff of Perdido was having a drink with friends across the state line in Florida. By the time that Charley Key returned to Perdido and heard about Carl Strickland's rampage, the Caskeys were surveying the damage. Key entered the house, gave a low whistle, looked at Oscar and said, "Mr. Strickland did this? You positive?"

"Yes," replied Oscar grimly.

"Is he still out there?"

"No, he's gone."

"How you know that for sure?"

Zaddie was on the stairs, sweeping glass and splinters down, step by step. Elinor came out of the kitchen, holding her bandaged daughter in her arms. Frances, pale and distracted, clung tightly to her mother's neck.

"I know it for sure," said Oscar, "because Elinor went out the front and sneaked around to the levee."

"I saw him take his guns and climb over the levee, and get in a boat," Elinor added with no particular friendliness toward the sheriff. "But he must have been drunk because the boat turned over in the water."

"Miz Caskey, you were foolish to go out there! Look at what he did in here. You might have got yourself shot!" cried Sheriff Key.

"I had a gun," Elinor said coldly. "And the fact was, we didn't see the law crawling all over the house trying to protect us. Oscar was firing at Carl from our window, and I went out to get him from behind."

"Did you shoot?"

"I didn't have to. The river got him. Sheriff," Elinor went on, laying ironic stress upon the title, "Oscar and I appreciate your dropping by—and we're glad you waited till most of the excitement was over, earlier we wouldn't have had much of a chance to speak—but could you excuse us now, please? I've got to finish bandaging my little girl."

"We're gone drag that river," said Charley Key importantly. "We're gone take care of Carl Strickland!"

"Charley," Oscar reminded him, "that's exactly what I asked you to do a few weeks ago, but you couldn't be bothered. You didn't want to do me any favors. Well, right now, Queenie Strickland, still black and blue, is upstairs crying in the bedroom. My little girl here is all cut up with glass. Our house has every damn window in it broken. And Carl Strickland is spinning round and round in the junction. Why don't you just go home and get some sleep?"

Zaddie swept a large pile of splintered wood and shattered glass between the balusters, and it fell to the hallway below with a musical crash and a cloud of dust.

Frances refused to return to the front room that night. Elinor was about to insist, but Zaddie interceded for the child. "Miss El'nor, she still scairt. Let her sleep with me."

"You don't have more than a three-quarter bed, Zaddie!"

"I don't care, Mama!" cried Frances desperately, and was reluctantly allowed to sleep in the room behind the kitchen. It was made clear to her, however, that this indulgence was solely on account of Carl Strickland's attack.

Toward dawn, when the house was quiet again, and the children were asleep, Elinor and Oscar lay awake in their bed. A breeze off the river—smelling of both the water and the red clay of the levee—blew through the windows that had been shattered by Carl Strickland's gunfire.

"Can't sleep, Oscar?"

"No, I cain't."

"Because of the excitement?"

"Yes, partly. I was thinking, Elinor."

"Thinking what?"

"Thinking that what you told old Charley Key was a lie."

"Course it was a lie," returned Elinor quickly. "You think I'm going to waste the truth on that nincompoop?"

"What happened out there with you and Carl?"

Elinor didn't immediately reply. She turned over in the bed and put her arm across Oscar's chest.

"What do you think happened, Oscar?"

Oscar lay still a few moments. The dawn dimly lighted the room now.

"I don't know," said Oscar. "What you told Charley Key was a lie—you didn't have a gun. When you came back into the house, your nightgown was dripping river water. Your bare feet had Perdido mud on 'em. I knew you had been in the water, because when you walked back in the house, you brought the *smell* of that river back here with you. How you're

75

ever gone be able to wear that gown again, I don't know."

Elinor snuggled closer to Oscar's side in the bed. She wound her arm around him and pressed her foot against his feet.

"Carl is dead," she said in a low voice. "I saw him drowned."

"I believe you," said Oscar. He lay staring at the ceiling. His arms were crossed behind his head on the pillow. "I wish," he went on, "that when I was shooting out the window here, that I had blown Carl's head off. That's what I wish. He was firing at this house! He could have hit Frances or you or Queenie or any of us. I would have walloped his head off if I could have gotten close enough. Elinor?"

"What?"

"Did you cause Carl Strickland to die?"

She rubbed her thumb against his neck. "Yes."

"I thought so," said Oscar, in a low sad voice. "How'd you do it? How'd you get close enough to him without him shooting you?"

Elinor drew her leg across Oscar's legs and pressed her foot beneath his ankles. She was wound tightly around him.

"What if I tell you?" she said. "Will you be mad?"

"Lord, no," he said softly. "I just said that *I* would have done it if I could have."

"It was dark," said Elinor. Her head was next to his on the pillow, and she spoke softly in his ear. "He couldn't see me. I swam under the water and overturned his boat as he was going across."

"Did he fight you?"

"No, he didn't even know I had done it," said Elinor.

"Were you *trying* to kill him?"

"Not really," said Elinor. "I just wanted to get those guns of his wet so it would ruin them. But he panicked once he was in the water. I saw him struggling, then I saw him drown."

"Did you try to save him then?"

"No," said Elinor. "I can't say that I did. Are you upset? Do you think I should have tried?"

"No, no," sighed Oscar. "I think you did just right. I just wish you hadn't had to do it. Is this gone be on your conscience?"

"I don't think so," said Elinor.

"Good," said Oscar, "'cause it shouldn't be. Carl brought this on himself. If you hadn't done it, it would only be a matter of time before he came back and killed one of us—Queenie, probably. She was the one he was really aiming for, I guess. It beats hell out me how some people can get matched up so badly. Poor old Queenie. She'll probably be glad to know Carl's gone. I don't think we should tell her that you killed him, though."

"Oscar, do you think badly of me? You know, some husbands might object to their wives going out in the night and killing people."

Oscar gave a short little laugh. "Not me. At least not until you start making a habit of it."

"You seem a little upset, though."

"I am," said Oscar. "It should have been me that went out and killed him, not you. I should have it on *my* conscience."

"How would you have done it?" laughed Elinor. "Oscar, you know you couldn't hit the levee with the rifle if you were standing twenty feet away. And you know you wouldn't go swimming in the Perdido in the middle of the night. It *had* to be me."

"I suppose. But listen, Elinor, if there's got to be any more killing in this family, you let *me* handle it for now on, you hear? Now, are you ready to try to get some sleep?"

"Not yet," she whispered.

Elinor had bathed, and her nightgown was fresh, but in that dawn following the death of Carl Strickland, Oscar found that the smell of the river was still caught in his wife's hair and in her limbs twined around his body.

Early the next morning, Bray and Oscar carried Queenie Strickland in a folding chair up to the top of the levee. Elinor brought her an umbrella against the sun, and then, joined by Zaddie, Frances, and Queenie's children, the entire household settled in to watch the dragging operation.

Within half an hour the state police came up with Carl's three rifles, which were identified by Queenie and Malcolm. Nothing could be found of Carl.

"Queenie," said James, who had joined the group on the levee, and now stood sympathetically at Queenie's side, "I'm so sorry."

"What for? What for, James?" cried Queenie. "Do you see what that man did to me? Do you know I may limp for the rest of my life? Do you know that I may be blind in one eye? Carl Strickland broke every single window in the back of Elinor and Oscar's house! It was a miracle nobody was killed. Have you seen the cuts on Frances's face?" Queenie held the umbrella above her head, twirling it in her agitation.

In the course of the morning, most of the rest of Perdido climbed the levee and walked along it to where Queenie sat watching the highway patrol and Sheriff Key in their boats below. Everyone knew that it was probably a pointless operation to drag the river. The current was swift, and the junction an inexorable maelstrom from which bodies were almost never recovered. Carl Strickland, though, had been a criminal, and it had been thought a good idea to attempt to prove his death.

Mary-Love made a brief appearance, hand-in-hand with Miriam. "Queenie," she said, "why'd you bring that man to town? Why didn't you leave him in Nashville? He was shooting off those guns at night! He could have got his aim wrong and shot my precious little Miriam in her room next door!"

"Those guns woke me up!" added Miriam in a petulant parenthesis.

"Mary-Love, I tell you, I didn't do it on purpose..."

"I sure hope they find him down there. Then we could be sure he'll never be coming back here again. I don't think Miriam and I got *one* wink of sleep after your husband started firing those guns! Just the echoes were hurting my ears!"

"I hope they find him too," said Queenie. She reached into the pocket of her dress and clacked together the two silver coins there. "Mary-Love, I want to see that man laid out on the bank of the river, and when I do, I'm gone slide right down this levee. See, I got these two quarters for Carl Strickland's eyes..."

Carl Strickland's body never was found, and there was no doubt in anyone's mind that he had drowned. His automobile was found parked in the live oak grove, his guns lay on the bed of the river, fragments of his boat washed up against the side of the levee down below the junction. At school Malcolm told prideful stories of his father's attempt to murder them all: "He was aiming right at my head, but I ducked! I wasn't gone let him shoot me!" Lucille pretended grief in order to be excused from participating in unwanted class activities.

The third day's dragging was desultory; only one policeman with a metal hook was being slowly propelled about by Bray in his boat. Queenie, watching from the levee, said to Ivey Sapp, who had brought up a pitcher of iced tea: "What do you think I ought to do about these quarters, Ivey? You think I should hold on to 'em?"

"Mr. Carl ain't gone be coming back, Miss Queenie."

"You sure?"

"They not never gone find him."

"I wish I could be sure!"

"Miss Queenie, you stand up here, and you throw

79

those quarters in the river. That'll keep down his bones."

With Ivey's assistance, Queenie stood from her chair and flung the coins into the muddy red water.

CHAPTER 35

The Test

Carl Strickland's two attempts to murder his wife had overshadowed, in Perdido's view, Wall Street's accumulating disasters. The stock market had crashed, but who in Perdido besides the mill owners had had much anyway? So no one paid much attention to the stock market business, but everyone in town breathlessly waited to see what would become of Queenie Strickland. She returned to her job at the mill. She flung open the doors of her house and never locked them at all now. She took her Malcolm and Lucille to the Ritz Theater every time there was a change in the bill and seemed to have as much fun as if she were a child herself, released from school a week early in May.

Queenie's recovery was rapid. The day after she certified her husband's death by flinging the two coins into the water, she returned to her own home. This evacuation was fortunate, for when Frances waked in Zaddie's bed the day after Carl had shot at the house, she had developed a sort of palsy of the hands and feet—uncommon in a seven-year-old—that Dr. Benquith diagnosed as incipient arthritis. Frances was out of school for a month. During that time her mother nursed her constantly without complaint. Queenie was certain that it had been brought on by Carl's attack on the house. Most of Perdido agreed with this, ignoring Dr. Benquith's assertion that arthritis was *not* brought on merely by an unpleasant experience.

More than a year passed, and Queenie's happiness became as conspicuous to the residents of Perdido as her troubles had been before. Now, however, that crisis of paper and faith in New York was beginning to have repercussions in Perdido. No one, not even the foresighted Caskeys, had anticipated how great and unsettling those effects were to prove.

The bank closed during Christmas week of 1930. Every white man and woman in town lost money.

Despite the fact that demand for wood and wood products was down, the mills continued to operate. There were no layoffs, though some days there wasn't enough work to be parceled out to the yard hands at the mills, and often the lumber business seemed no more than a charitable exercise on the parts of the Turks and the Caskeys.

Perdido seemed to suffer less than many parts of the country. Or perhaps it just seemed that way; Perdido was, after all, accustomed to hardship. The prosperity of the twenties had made only mincing steps toward rural Alabama, and when she whirled about and fled with a flash of skirts from the rest of the country, Perdido had enjoyed so little of her company that it scarcely missed her. The privations of the Civil War seemed recent, and there were old black men and women in Baptist Bottom who had been born slaves. Mary-Love Caskey and Manda Turk both had been born during the humiliating privations of Reconstruction. But, certainly there was less to go around now. Grady Henderson's "fancy goods store" dwindled to a simple grocery, and Leo Benquith bartered chickens, pork loins, and quarts of shelled peas for his services as a physician. At the school there was a greater incidence of ringworm and rickets. Ample and decent food soared beyond the means of poorer families. Several downtown shops closed, and the Osceola Hotel would have shut its doors had not Henry and Oscar lent the Moyes enough money to keep it going. The Osceola was needed by the mills for the housing of the few buyers who came in from the hard-hit North. Collections in the churches were sparser than in previous years, though attendance was up. Perhaps for the same reason, the Ritz Theater—including the colored folks' balcony— was filled nearly every night.

Yet the Caskeys remained solvent. Oscar's diversification of the operations of the mill insured that some portion of the enterprise remained profitable. Mary-Love's money had fortuitously been invested in things that were not so much affected by the Depression. There were, however, no more jaunts to Mobile and Birmingham for the purchase of new tablecloths and dresses. Mary-Love wore her old outfits, or commissioned straitened Miz Daughtry to make her new ones. Oscar hung about the mill all day with very little to do.

James Caskey suffered more than Mary-Love. Most of his stocks had lost much or all of their value, and the company yielded almost no return at all. Despite the unaccustomed financial ills, he was happy again. At sixty, he actually enjoyed the slower pace of the mill, which rolled along with very little help from him. He and Queenie were fast friends now. They lunched together every day at his house and spent the afternoon talking in the office. He quietly spent his evenings at home, listening to the radio. Danjo often sat on the sofa next to him, looking through books and asking his uncle's help with difficult words. James's wants were few, and it was his delight to take care of those who needed taking care of. When Roxie went for groceries, he made certain she bought enough to feed not only himself and Danjo, but her husband and her four children as well. Queenie received a raise almost every month and was always paid in cash out of James's pocket. Every week at Vanderbilt, Grace's female chums gasped in astonishment as *another* sheaf of five-dollar bills arrived in a plain envelope. James did almost nothing for himself, and scarcely could be persuaded to buy himself a new suit at Easter. He made no more purchases of porcelain figures or sterling silver cakeservers, saying—reasonably enough—that his house was full of such stuff anyway.

Only Oscar and Elinor encountered real difficulties. Oscar was still in debt on the land he had purchased from Tom DeBordenave, and because there was so little cutting, his income from the land was severely reduced. His meager return went to the bank in Pensacola. Oscar and Elinor still lived on Oscar's salary alone.

In the spring of 1931, the bank called in Oscar's loan. That afternoon, without saying a word to anyone, Oscar drove to Pensacola and obtained an interview with the president of the bank. Oscar was told that the bank itself was in difficulties. The loan had been called in as a measure against an involuntary closing. However, the Caskeys had done a great deal of business with the institution over the years, so it was therefore agreed—after a hurried meeting of the trustees—that only half of Oscar's outstanding debt need be brought in.

That evening Oscar visited his mother. Closeted in her room with the door closed, he asked her to lend him one hundred and eleven thousand dollars to preserve his investment, his financial well-being, the honor of the Caskey name, and the future of the mill. She wouldn't do it.

"Oscar, I told you not to buy that land."

"You didn't, Mama," replied Oscar calmly. "You didn't even find out about it until later."

"If you had had the courtesy to speak to me about it beforehand, I would have told you not to buy it. I'm glad that the bank is doing this. You have no business being saddled with all that land."

"Mama, it's got *trees* on it. Every single acre has been planted with yellow pine."

"Oscar," she said, "James and I own two hundred thousand acres of land in Escambia County, Monroe County, and this county. Every one of those two hundred thousand acres is planted with yellow pine, and longleaf pine, and slash pine. And when was the last time we had order for ten board feet of lumber? Was it day before yesterday, or was it three weeks ago? Lord, Oscar, we cain't even *begin* to harvest what we've got now!"

"Mama, are you deliberately misunderstanding me?" Oscar asked. He glanced out his mother's bedroom window at his own home next door. He could see his wife and daughter sitting on the swing on the sleeping porch. They sat beneath a red-fringed lamp, and Elinor was reading to Frances in a soft voice he could hear as a murmur.

"What do you mean?"

"I mean that I am asking you to lend me the money for my own sake, not for the mill's. That land is all I've got in the world. If I lose it then I don't have anything."

"You have your house."

"Mama, that house belongs to you. You have never given me the deed," replied Oscar sadly.

"You have your work at the mill."

"Yes, I do," returned Oscar. "And I have near about worked myself to death for that mill. Every penny of the money I've made has gone to you and James— now wait, I'm not complaining, I was glad to do it. It's the Caskey mill, and I'm a Caskey, but, Mama, it sure looks to me like you might give me a little something to pay me back for making life so easy for you in these hard times."

"I don't call a hundred and eleven thousand dollars 'a little something.'"

"Mama, you've got the money. I know you have. I know you've got it, because I *made* that money for you. I wrote the checks and put it in your account in Mobile."

"I'm not gone throw good money after bad. Oscar, you don't need that land. Let it go. Let the bank take it back. They had no business lending you money for it in the first place. I'd even like to hear what you used for collateral. You give 'em Frances maybe? The way you gave Miriam to me in exchange for your house?"

Oscar felt embarrassed for the cruelty in his mother's words.

"All right, Mama," he said, rising. His voice and his face were stony.

"You let that land go, you have no business owning property."

"Whatever you say, Mama."

He stood still, looking at her, where she sat in a rocker by the window. Over her shoulder, he could see Elinor and Frances in the soft light of the lamp. He could hear Elinor's voice with that of his daughter blend, as together they read a poem out of the book. The evening wind was damp and cool. The water oak branches creaked high above the ground. Mary-Love Caskey grew restive beneath her son's gaze.

"Only reason you're doing this is 'cause of Elinor," she said. "If it wasn't for Elinor, you'd be perfectly happy doing what you've always done. She's the one made sure you went over your head in debt for that land that's not ever gone do you one bit of good."

"Mama, is that what you really think?"

"It is. And it's the truth."

"Do you really hate Elinor that much?"

"Shhh! She's gone hear you."

"Do you hate Elinor, Mama, hate her so much you'd send me into bankruptcy just to hurt her?"

"You're gone be all right, Oscar. You think I'd let you starve?"

"No, I don't," said Oscar. "But I do think you'd like to see Elinor and Frances and me kneeling on your back steps, waiting for Miriam to bring us a plate of food."

For a moment, Mary-Love was silent. Her son had never spoken to her in such a manner, and yet there was no anger or emotion in his voice.

"Oscar," she went on as if he had said nothing, "all this is gone teach you a lesson."

"Bankruptcy?"

"It's gone teach you not to try to do things over your head."

Oscar laughed one brief, mirthless laugh. "Mama, I'm not going into bankruptcy. I'm gone keep that land."

"What do you mean?"

"I mean that if you won't help me, James will."

"He won't!"

"Mama, James co-signed the loan. If I default, the bank will go to him for the money. You know that if that happens, James will sell everything he owns to pay it off. It'll be hard for him, and I hate to put him through it, but he'll see that the bank is paid. Then I'll owe *him* the money instead of owing it to the bank."

"Lord, Oscar, if this is true, then why in the world did you come to me?"

"Because you're my mama and you're rich and I have worked for you all my life. I *made* you rich, and it was time that you did a little something to help me."

"I'll help you, Oscar, I'd help you with anything."

"No, Mama," said Oscar. He had gone to the door, and leaned his back against it, twisting the knob in

87

his hands. "You wouldn't. You just said you wouldn't. You just said you had rather send me into bankruptcy than help me out—even though, in the end, you'd be hurting the mill and James and yourself. You'd do all that just to spite Elinor and spite me for marrying her."

"You did this as a test, Oscar! You didn't have any intention of trying to borrow from me, you just wanted to see if I'd give in, that's all! That's despicable of you, that's—"

"No, Mama," said Oscar, shaking his head, and his soft voice overcame her angry tone. "I really needed you this time. James had helped me before, and now I wanted *you* to help me, but you wouldn't do it. That makes me real sad, Mama..."

"What are you gone do, Oscar?" Mary-Love asked, in a low, mistrustful voice. The test might not be over yet.

"I'm gone borrow the money from James. I told you that."

"Are you sure he's got it? Are you sure he'll give it to you?"

"Yes," said Oscar. "I'm sure he will. Nobody's gone default. I'll come through it, and someday I'll pay James back. And the Caskey mill will come through, and Mama, you're just gone get richer and richer. And when you die, we're gone fill your coffin with hundred-dollar bills, and we're gone put you in the cemetery right next to Genevieve—and I guess you'll have the time of your life, with Genevieve to keep you company and all that money to keep you warm."

After her son had gone home Mary-Love sat in her darkened room and looked out of her window. She saw Oscar appear on the screened porch next door, saw him kiss Elinor and take up Frances. She heard his murmuring voice as he read to his daughter.

* * *

The next day Luvadia Sapp knocked on Elinor's door. "Morning, Luvadia," Elinor said in greeting. "Is there something you need?"

"Miss Mary-Love tell me to give you this," replied Luvadia, holding out a folded document with a red seal. That morning in the office of the clerk of probate, Mary-Love had signed over the house to Oscar and Elinor.

CHAPTER 36

At the River's Source

In dealing with her son's request for a loan, Mary-Love had not understood that there are some acts that are unforgivable. Oscar had been only half right in telling his mother that she wanted him to go bankrupt to spite Elinor; she also wanted to make certain that her son would always remain dependent. If Mary-Love had realized that James would lend Oscar the money—and she *should* have realized that—then she would not have had a moment's hesitation in helping out her son. In that way, she also realized later, she might have maintained her position as the Caskey cornucopia.

When she had refused her son, Oscar went to James, who sold off a sheaf of bonds and handed the money over to Oscar without a murmur or a reproach. Half of Oscar's outstanding debt to the bank was immediately canceled, and his monthly payments on the remainder were consequently eased. He and Elinor were left with more than they had

had to get along with formerly. It was true that Oscar was now heavily indebted to his uncle, as well as to the bank, but James would rather have gone bankrupt himself than inconvenience his nephew by demanding repayment of this sum.

Oscar felt that he had outwitted his mother. Yet his victory did not make him forgiving toward her. He had told no one of her refusal to help him, but now he barely spoke to Mary-Love. When she lay in wait for him on her front porch, and beckoned to him as he got out of his automobile, he'd only reply, in his blandest voice, "Hey, Mama, sorry I cain't come over right now, got to go inside. Elinor wants me!" When she called him on the telephone he would politely answer any question she put to him, but would volunteer nothing more, and always rang off as quickly as possible with an unabashedly fabricated excuse. They would sit in the same pew at church—the Caskeys had always sat together—but Oscar called a halt to his attending Mary-Love's Sunday afternoon dinners. After services he and Elinor and Frances would usually drive to Pensacola for dinner at the Hotel Palafox.

Oscar's repudiation was particularly painful to Mary-Love because it wasn't public; she therefore couldn't represent herself as a martyr to Oscar's cruelty. She knew he never said a word against her. He was always polite when she spoke to him, but nothing on earth would persuade him to have anything to do with her. Mary-Love at last felt compelled to speak to Elinor. She knocked on the door of the big house next door one morning an hour or so before Oscar was expected home for the noon meal.

"I won't stay," Mary-Love assured her daughter-in-law. "I won't even come inside. But, Elinor, can you sit out here on the porch with me a minute?"

"Of course," said Elinor, and the two women placed themselves in facing rockers. Across the road from the Caskey houses was a large, fenced pecan orchard, with a number of Holstein heifers grazing in it. No pair of those cows appeared more phlegmatic or imperturbable than Mary-Love Caskey and her daughter-in-law, as they sat on the porch and prepared to do battle.

"Elinor, you got to talk to Oscar."

"About what?"

"About the way he's treating me."

Elinor looked at her mother-in-law without expression. "I don't understand."

"You know what I'm talking about," Mary-Love continued, annoyed that her honesty should not be reciprocated.

"He hasn't been visiting you the way he used to," Elinor admitted. "I've noticed that."

"And he's told you why, hasn't he?"

"No," returned Elinor. "He hasn't said a word."

"Well, didn't you ask?"

"Whatever it is, it's between you and Oscar. I didn't think it was any of my business."

"Elinor, I came to ask you to help me patch things up. It hurts me the way he treats me. I'm embarrassed for Oscar's sake. And I think *you* ought to speak to him about it."

"What do you want me to say?"

"Tell him that people see how he treats me. And people think ill of him for it. If he doesn't watch out, people are going to turn on him for acting toward me the way he does. He should put things back the way they used to be."

"Why should he?" Elinor asked innocently. "I mean, what reason should I give him?"

"Because the whole town is talking, like I said!"

"You're telling me that you want Oscar to patch things up for *his* sake, not yours? That is, you don't care one way or the other?"

"No, that's not what I mean at all!" said Mary-Love. "I *do* care! Oscar hurts me, the way he treats me. We all used to be so happy!" she sighed.

"Miss Mary-Love, I don't think I'd go so far as to say *that!* But I will speak to Oscar, I will tell him what you said, and I will tell him that he is injuring his reputation in town by his treatment of you."

"Elinor, what do you think about it?"

"I think it's between you and Oscar and that it's none of my business. I'll speak to Oscar purely as a favor to you."

Mary-Love Caskey loathed favors done her. She sought desperately for a device that would make Elinor see things differently and relieve her of any possible obligation to her daughter-in-law. "Yes, but wouldn't you like to see Oscar and me on good terms again? Things would be much easier for you then, too."

"Miss Mary-Love, it makes not one bit of difference in the world to me what goes on between you and your son. Oscar is a grown man, and Oscar can do exactly what he wants. I think that in the end that will be what Oscar does do about it: exactly what he wants."

"Elinor," said Mary-Love, halting the rocker and looking her daughter-in-law straight in the eye, "you sure you don't know what any of this is about?"

"I haven't the foggiest idea."

"Elinor, you can sit there and say that, but I'm just not so sure I can believe you."

"I have no reason to lie to you, Miss Mary-Love. I'll speak to Oscar." With this unsatisfactory assurance, Mary-Love departed.

When Oscar came home for lunch, Elinor dutifully reported his mother's visit, pleas, and exhortations.

Oscar looked at his wife across the table, and said, "Elinor, Mama did something to me that I don't know if I can ever forgive her for. One thing sure, I haven't forgiven her yet. And it's not that I don't want to, because I do, it's that I just *cain't.* And that's what you can tell her."

94

"Oscar, I refuse to act as a go-between. I wish you'd tell your mother that yourself."

"All right, I suppose I'll have to. Elinor, did Mama tell you what all this was about?"

"No, she didn't."

"Aren't you curious?"

"If you want to tell me, then tell me. If you don't want to tell me, then I don't intend to ask."

"Well, then," said Oscar, after a pause, "I guess I better go on and tell you." Oscar told his wife about Mary-Love's refusal to give him any money and about their confrontation. Elinor made no comment. "What are you thinking?" her husband asked.

"I'm thinking that it's a wonder you speak to her at all. It's one thing for her to hate me, but it's something else for her to injure herself and the entire family."

To this, her husband made rueful agreement. "Someday," he said sadly, "we are gone look out the dining room window and see the barnyard fowl lining up on Mama's rain gutter."

"What do you mean?"

"Someday," Oscar explained, "Mama's chickens are gone come home to roost."

Mary-Love intercepted her son as he left the house on his way back to work a half hour later. She had been sitting on her front porch, and she hurried over just as he was getting into his car.

"Oscar, did Elinor speak to you?"

"Yes, ma'am."

"Well? Did she tell you how you were being talked about all over town because of your treatment of me?"

Oscar put his hand on the hood of the car. "Mama," he said softly, "that's just like you."

"What is?"

"I think it would kill you just to come out and say, 'Oscar, what you're doing is hurting *me*.' Instead you're saying, 'Oscar, I don't care about me, but you're

95

hurting yourself.' You always have to be the one who does the favors. Well, Mama, if it's not hurting you, then that's fine. Go on back inside the house. Leave me alone."

During this unhappy time for Mary-Love and Oscar, James Caskey and Danjo Strickland were getting along wonderfully well. Now seven, Danjo felt secure in his position. His father was dead and unlikely to claim him again. His mother seemed content only to visit him, though this she did nearly every day. James had recently purchased a car, and Danjo had been staked as no part of that transaction. Grace returned from Vanderbilt for summers and holiday vacations. Twice James and Danjo had driven up to Nashville to visit her.

Grace loved the boy for James's sake, and whenever she saw him the first thing she invariably asked was, "Are you taking care of my daddy?"

Danjo always nodded vigorously and replied proudly, "He said he couldn't get along without me!"

"I don't think he could!" Grace always cried, hugging her father until the breath was nearly squeezed out of him.

It seemed that all had worked out for the best. Grace had abandoned her father, but James never tired of saying, "I was so lonesome when Grace left that I went down to the Ben Franklin and bought me a little boy. He cost me a dollar fifty-nine, but he's been worth every penny!"

Grace was happy at school. This was always evident to James when he and Danjo visited her in Nashville. Her room was crammed with furniture James had bought. She had pennants on the walls. Oriental parasols opened and suspended from the ceiling had electric light bulbs hidden behind them. There were layers of carpet on the floor and two palms and a Victrola sat in one corner.

James could also see that Grace was very popular.

Every time he walked into the room a bevy of young women who had been lounging there jumped up and shook his hand, hugged Danjo, and all cried out, "What'd you bring Grace *this* time, Mr. Caskey?" Besides the sheaf of five-dollar bills in the unmarked envelope, he usually had a vast package tied up in brown paper and string, sitting downstairs in the hallway. Grace would unwrap it, and a pleasant half hour was then spent in trying to find a place to put whatever it was James had brought. James always took Grace out to dinner alone on Friday night, but on Saturday night, he treated almost the entire dormitory at a restaurant. Nobody on earth was blessed with a sweeter father than Grace Caskey. No man's daughter was better loved than Grace Caskey.

"Have you made acquaintance with the man of your dreams?" was James's invariable question when he and Grace were alone together.

"Ugh!" Grace always cried. "Why should I want to do that?"

"So you can settle down and get married, that's why," James would return mildly.

"I don't want to get married, Daddy. I'm having a good time. I don't think I've let myself be introduced to one single man on this campus."

James would laugh. "Well, darling, if you don't even let 'em know your name, how are they supposed to propose to you?"

"I don't want them to! And I'll beat 'em over the head if they try."

This did not seem such an idle threat. At college, Grace Caskey had discovered the delights of physical culture, and she had a closetful of white tennis dresses, white boating clothes, white gymnasium pants, and white football sweaters. Her many handsome sporting outfits began to crowd out her regular wardrobe. Her favorite pastime was rowing, and she was unanimously elected captain of the girls' crew team when she was a junior. She also ran track and played basketball, where the Caskey height stood her in good stead. In this rough-and-tumble atmosphere, Grace acquired a forthrightness and heartiness of demeanor that was shocking to those in Perdido who remembered her only as a slight, somewhat diffident, whiny child. Grace had become strong enough actually to lift her father bodily from the floor, and now whenever they met, she did it.

The summers of Grace's college years were particularly pleasant for James Caskey, for Grace returned at the beginning of June, and didn't leave again until the beginning of September. He always told her to go off and have a good time and not think about him, but Grace would only reply, "Daddy, I miss you so much up there, sometimes I think I ought to pack you in my trunk and keep you with me. You don't think I'm gone do anything in my summers but sit on your front porch and rock, do you?"

"Won't you be lonely?"

But Grace was hardly lonely during these summers, for she sent out invitations to all her friends to come and visit her in the pokiest town on earth, Perdido, Alabama. Evidently Grace herself was sufficient draw, because the girls came and stayed for days or weeks. James's house was filled with young women and young women's clothing and young women's hearty voices and heartier laughter. When there wasn't any more room at James's, the girls stayed at Elinor's, or even at Queenie's. They never stayed at Mary-Love's, who disapproved of any member of the Caskey family maintaining a friendship. The girls rowed on the Perdido, took cooking lessons from Roxie, went in a bevy to the Ritz Theater, played boisterous tag among the water oaks, and visited Lake Pinchona relentlessly to swim, feed the alligator, and annoy the monkey. They made impromptu excursions to Mobile or down to the Pensacola beaches or up to Brewton to pick scuppernongs. They would travel over to Fort Mims to play hide-and-seek among the ruins of Alabama's first capital, have picnics in the green fields along the Alabama River, or make daring raft excursions down the turbulent Styx. Danjo was often picked up squealing and flung into the back of Grace's Pontiac with a cry of, "Danjo, we're kidnapping you and you're never gone see Mr. Caskey again!"

"Grace's girls," as they came quickly to be known around town, were a formidable bunch, certainly too much for the few college men that Perdido produced to handle. Young Perdido manhood found companionship with the girls occasionally on the dance floor at the lake, but was otherwise contemptuously ignored. The girls made much of James Caskey and Danjo Strickland, so that the boy and his uncle—accustomed to the winter quietness of Perdido and only each other for company—were always quite bewildered by the energy, the lightheartedness, and the noise of it all.

In the spring of 1933, Grace Caskey graduated from Vanderbilt with a degree in history, and five letters in women's athletics. Her father had never asked her what she intended to do after graduation, but once he had said, "Grace, if you ever decide on anything, let me know, will you?" With a particularly good friend, Grace applied for a position at a girl's school in Spartanburg, South Carolina, and was overjoyed that they were both offered jobs. Her friend was to teach English literature, and Grace was in charge of the gymnasium. Grace's girls came down to Perdido that summer as in the past, but the time was tinged with melancholy. Already some of the girls were engaged, and it was obvious to them all that these happy months of laughter and company could never be repeated. This summer, Grace's girls paid particular attention to Frances, who seemed frailer than ever, after her bout with arthritis two years before. The activity and the attention seemed to do much to lift the eleven-year-old's spirits. Mir-

99

iam tried to be contemptuous of the intimacy that Frances enjoyed with the co-eds; mostly, however, she was angry that she was so rarely asked to take part in their frequent excursions.

Melancholy seasons end quicker than happy ones, and Grace's girls broke up, never again to be joined together. Grace remained alone with her family another week before James would drive her up to Spartanburg and see her installed there.

On the second of September, 1933, the weather in Perdido was still brutally hot, but James Caskey was already pining beneath the weight of autumn when his daughter would leave him for good.

Grace said, "Daddy, why don't just you and I go out in the boat this afternoon? Let me take you for a ride up the Perdido."

"Who'll take care of Danjo?"

"Roxie's here."

"I mean, who'll take care of Danjo when you and I and that little green boat all get washed down to the junction?"

Grace laughed merrily. "Daddy, don't you realize that I'm strong enough to avoid the junction? Just like Elinor can. Besides, we won't even go that way, we'll go upstream."

"Darling, I tell you what—why don't you take Frances? She's gone miss you so much, and this way you can get to talk to her alone for a while."

Grace thought this a fine idea. Without a moment's hesitation she went over and stood underneath the screened porch and called up to Elinor.

"Mama's not here," said Frances, leaning on the rail and looking down.

"Where'd she go?"

"She went swimming, it was so hot."

"In the Perdido?" asked Grace.

"Uh-hunh."

"I didn't really want your mama anyway, Frances. I wanted to ask you if you wanted to take a little ride in the boat. You think your mother would mind if I took you out on the water?"

"Not one bit! She's always *wanting* me to go out on the river!"

"Then come on down, and we'll see if we cain't sneak up on her and surprise her in the water."

Grace's boat was tied to a tree where the levee ended in a steep slope a hundred yards or so upstream. Grace shoved the boat halfway into the water and let Frances climb in so that she wouldn't have to wet her feet. Then she pushed the boat farther out and jumped in herself. The current immediately began dragging the boat downstream, and Frances nervously called out "Whoooa!"

Grace paddled hard against the current, and after only a few moments they were headed upstream. The Perdido was fed by many hundreds of tiny branches of water, most of which were so insubstantial and ephemeral they hadn't even the strength to dig channels for themselves across the floor of the forest. Along the course of the uninhabited upper river, these freshets slipped rapidly over beds of decaying pine needles and oak leaves and poured into the Perdido with low, furtive gurglings. As Grace and Frances ascended the river, this was the only sound to be heard. They might have been the water voices of small gilled creatures, stationed sentrylike along the banks of the ever-narrowing river, announcing the upstream progress of the young woman and the young girl in their boat.

"I don't see Mama," said Frances. "Maybe she went the other direction."

As they proceeded up the river, far past any point that was familiar to either Grace or Frances, the Perdido grew shallow and quiet. The freshets, like sentinels whose commander has been apprised of the approach of strangers, had now fallen silent. Once Grace raised her paddle high and brought it down swiftly on a water moccasin gliding past them. It

101

was not because they were in danger, but she followed the general philosophy that poisonous things, like gentlemen who made proposals of marriage, ought to be beaten over the head.

"I've never been this far up," Frances remarked with wonder at the wildness of the country through which they were traveling. They seemed far from Perdido.

"Look," said Grace pointing upward, "those are wild orchids on the branches of those oaks. It's so lonely up here..."

"Have you ever been all the way up to the source?"

"No, I haven't. I've never even heard of anybody going all that way—I guess somebody must have, but nobody's ever told me. Frances, shall we try to find it?"

"What if it's twenty miles or something?"

"It's not. 'Cause if it were, Highway 31 would cross it and I know it doesn't, so the source cain't be more than five or six miles away."

"But if this old river starts winding around..."

"I don't mind paddling. Only thing is, at some point we may have to get out and walk."

"I don't mind that," said Frances. So Grace continued to ply her paddle. The river narrowed until it was no more than a creek, then only a branch. It never, however, lost its muddy red color. Even with Grace's paddle often gouging pebbles and mud from the bed, they were never able to see to the bottom. The trees that overhung the little stream, shading it from the sun, were mostly hardwoods, not pine at all. The forest was thick here, its floor spongy with fallen trees and rotting leaves.

"Frances, you know what? I don't think this land has ever been cut."

"Really? Who does it belong to?"

"I've been trying to figure, and you know what I think?"

"What?"

"I think this used to be Tom DeBordenave's property, and it's some of the land that he sold to your daddy. That's about what I make out."

As Grace made this observation, she engineered a sharp turn around a massive fallen oak that had at one point rerouted the stream. Ahead of them was a small muddy pool of reddish water, its surface quivering and suffused with ripples. All around it was a stand of tall, gray, massive water oaks—far taller than those Elinor had years ago planted in the sandy Caskey yards. The slender trunks gravely swayed in the slight breeze and masses of leathery leaves quaked in their hundred-foot crowns. The ground was a thicket of rotting fallen limbs with no vegetation except the scaly green fungus that seemed the parasite peculiar to the species.

"This is it," murmured Grace. "This is where the Perdido starts."

There was something solemn in the place. The tall, sentinellike trees seemed almost ominous; and the little red pool that was the source of the Perdido looked threatening with its nervous, rippling activity. Even the birds seemed to have abandoned the place. The sun fell behind the water oaks as Grace placed her paddle in the crotch of two branches of the fallen tree, and held the boat stationary. It seemed to Frances that she feared to advance into the pool that was the river's source.

"Grace," said Frances after a few moments, "don't you think we ought to turn back? Mama wouldn't want us to be on the river after dark."

"It won't take us any time at all to get home. I won't have to paddle at all, except to steer us clear of sandbars. You know," she said in a lower voice, "it's a little scary up here. I used to think Perdido was out of the way, but Perdido is nothing compared to *this* place..."

Grace and Frances continued to stare in silence. The spot seemed divorced from the countryside they

103

knew well. It seemed absurd to speak of Oscar's owning such a place, or to think that this glade and pool and stand of water oak might even appear on a map. The source of the Perdido seemed outside all that; seemed to be part of something that rose above lumber leases and land sales and geological surveys. It seemed impossible that a state road or a county bridge or some tenant farmer's shack or some Cherokee's liquor still might be anywhere close by, yet both Grace and Frances knew that all of these were situated no more than a mile or two away. All civilization seemed separated from this strange spot by space and time. Suddenly, Grace gave a little shudder. The atmosphere was abruptly altered. With the paddle, she pushed away from the tree and set the boat back into the current of the river. As she did so, the commotion on the surface of the water of the pool seemed to grow as if a greater amount of water, or of a very different kind had been released from below.

Grace glanced at Frances. She saw that terror had spread over her cousin's face. Frances's body was trembling feverishly, and she convulsively grasped the sides of the boat. "Hurry," she whispered. "Please Grace, hurry."

Grace paddled energetically and in another moment they were around the sharp bend around the fallen tree. With that, Frances felt a bit calmer, and she could not resist a glance back at the muddy red pool that was the source of the Perdido. In a moment, it was beyond her sight, obscured by another bend of the river. But in that moment, slowly breaking the surface of the water, Frances Caskey saw a face, wide and pale green, with bulging eyes and no nose at all. Something about it—despite the horror of it—was familiar to her.

"Mama," she whispered, but Grace did not hear.

CHAPTER 37

Upstairs

Grace was silent on the journey back down the Perdido. As they were carried along by the current of the ever-widening river, Frances sat rigidly in the front of the boat, facing away from her cousin.

"Frances, are you all right?" Grace asked anxiously more than once.

Frances nodded weakly, but did not turn around.

After Grace had tied the boat to the tree near the end of the levee she discovered that Frances was unable to walk. Grace had to carry her all the way back to the house.

Elinor still had not returned, but Zaddie took one look at the child in Grace's arms, and said, with ominous significance, "That's the arthritis again."

Frances was taken upstairs and put into bed. Grace sat at her side until Elinor returned, a half hour later.

Grace was nearly in tears. "Elinor, it's my fault!"

"Don't be silly," said Elinor sternly. "Dr. Benquith said it could come back at any time."

The child lay in a feverish doze. When she woke late that night, the palsy in her legs had got no better.

In her last days in Perdido, Grace Caskey was convinced that the excursion to the source of the Perdido was solely responsible for the recurrence of Frances's crippling ailment. Elinor, Oscar, James, and Frances herself did what they could to assure Grace that it was not so.

Grace left for Spartanburg, and when she returned at Christmas, Frances still had not got up from her bed. Dr. Benquith had wanted to send the child to Sacred Heart in Pensacola, or even to one of the big hospitals in Cincinnati, but Elinor would not hear of this. "I'm going to continue to nurse my child until she's better."

Nothing seemed to ease Frances's pain but warm baths. For two hours every morning, two hours every afternoon, and for an hour in the evening after supper, Elinor sat at the side of the bathtub, sponging water over Frances's helpless limbs. The child seemed always weary. Sometimes her eyelids twitched with some pain that had registered in her brain, but she never complained. Elinor gave up playing bridge; she no longer went to church. She didn't like to leave her daughter. There was never the air of the martyr about her, never the sense that she was sacrificing anything for Frances. On her good days, the girl was carried out onto the screened porch and laid in a little cot-bed.

But Frances's good days were infrequent. At times she appeared to have no mind whatsoever. She lay uncomplaining in her bed, twitching violently when overtaken by the palsy, perfectly still at all other times. Looking at her clenched hands, Oscar was certain that Frances was tense and bitter. Elinor said that contraction of her fingers into uncontrolled claws was only the arthritis, as were her in-turning, twisted feet. Occasionally the girl made an effort to reply when she was spoken to directly, but more often she did not. Nothing held her interest. Nothing could bring emotion into her face, not a Christmas stocking nailed to the hearth in her room, not a cake with lighted candles on her birthday, not Malcolm's Fourth of July firecrackers. When it was time for her bath, Elinor lifted her daughter from the bed. Oscar hated to see this more than anything else about the sickness. He saw that Frances wanted desperately to clasp her arms about her mother's neck, but all those muscles seemed atrophied or recalcitrant, and the thin pathetic limbs hung limply down Elinor's back.

Frances missed the sixth and seventh grades. Elinor borrowed books from the school and kept up with her daughter's lessons, but how much of her mother's reading Frances comprehended, no one could be certain. Oscar and Elinor's household was completely altered during Frances's enfeeblement. Elinor withdrew from Perdido society. She became a voluntary drudge to her daughter's meager comfort. Oscar ventured to object: "Let Zaddie do some of the work, Elinor. You act like it was your fault that Frances got sick again. It wasn't anybody's fault."

Elinor paid no attention to her husband. She rose at five and on winter mornings built a coal fire for Frances. She kept it going all day. When she wasn't bathing Frances, she was reading to her, or feeding her, or simply sitting at the side of the bed rubbing alcohol onto Frances's wasting limbs. Before each bath, Elinor took two pails and walked through the pine forest to the west of the house and around the end of the levee. She filled the pails with water from the river and brought them back to the house. They were warmed in a great pot on the stove and carried upstairs. One of these pails was added directly to Frances's bath; the other was sponged over Frances's twitching limbs. Oscar and Dr. Benquith couldn't understand this worthless treatment, but there was no talking Elinor out of it. When Mary-Love heard of it, she declared that Frances must be red as an Indian by now with all that Perdido water poured over her.

This for Frances was a blurry time of confusion and weakness. Her brain seemed to have taken on the same palsy as her limbs. She slept and woke and ate and heard her mother read all in a state of only partial awareness. She sat in the bathtub with equal lassitude and low consciousness. She seemed always feverish, always dreaming. She was never certain whether she had fully awakened after that trip up to the source of the river with Grace. The only time total consciousness approached was when Elinor lifted her out of the bath. She felt the muddy Perdido water wash off her and drip back into the bathtub. This was the only thing in Frances's life that was sharp, except for the pain that racked her limbs. Hours faded, days drifted by, season slipped into season, and she did not know whether Thanksgiving had just passed, or whether it was already summer. Everything she felt was dreamlike and vague, except for the pain in her legs and arms—and the water of the Perdido slipping from her body.

Eventually, Frances Caskey's health began to improve. Dr. Benquith called it remission. Mary-Love sententiously claimed it was her prayers. Ivey Sapp said it was red Perdido water.

Frances's hands became less clawed. Once more she was able to hold a pencil long enough to write a note to Grace in Spartanburg, to say how well she was coming along. She could lift a glass without spilling its contents. She could use a fork, though it would be some time before she regained the strength and agility to employ a knife at the same time. On the porch, she sat in a wheelchair. In the spring of 1936, nearly three years after she was stricken, she was able to take a few steps by grasping pieces of furniture or woodwork and pulling herself along.

Frances missed three years of school, but she had learned from her mother's excellent tutelage after all, so when she returned she was put back only one grade. But physically she had grown very little in her illness. The first Sunday that she returned with Elinor to the Caskey pew, Mary-Love ungenerously remarked, "Why, Frances, you aren't hardly any bigger than the last time I saw you."

In the three years of illness, Mary-Love Caskey hadn't once visited her granddaughter, though on still summer nights she could hear Frances next door whimper from her pain. Mary-Love claimed this neglect was only a reluctance to intrude. She said she had feared that Frances would be disturbed by too many visitors, but this excuse fooled no one. If Oscar had ever felt inclined to make things up with his mother, any such feeling was now completely gone. His mother's treatment of Frances seemed a piece of conspicuous cruelty to the child.

Miriam, who had grown tall and thin, said to her sister, "Grandmama said whatever you had was probably infectious, and that's why I never went over to see you. How on earth are you going to catch up, after being out of school for three years? I don't imagine you'll *ever* catch up, really..."

There were other changes, besides her sister's height, that Frances noticed. Perdido looked as if it were falling into decay. Fifteen houses in Baptist Bottom had burned one New Year's Eve, and no one had yet bothered to clear away the rubble. A line of stores downtown was boarded up, and the windows had been smashed. The ragged curtains in the open windows of the Osceola Hotel blew in the wind.

Frances often sat in the kitchen with Zaddie, and was astonished by the number of black children who came to the lattice door and knocked softly. Zaddie always had a plate of cornbread or a part of a ham or a slab of bacon for them to take home. Next day the child would return with the plate, and a thank you from its mother.

Frances asked her mother about this.

"Nobody has anything, darling. I wish we could afford to do more, but even we don't have what we used to."

Frances shook her head; she understood nothing about money.

"We'll be all right," Elinor assured her. "But while you were upstairs"—Elinor always referred to her daughter's illness by that euphemism—"your daddy had some hard times out at the mill. He had to let people go."

"Is it all right now?"

"I don't know. We'll have to wait and see. Henry Turk, it looks like, is going under. He's going to have to sell out."

"To whom?"

Elinor shook her head. "To us, I'd like to think. He hasn't got anything left except his land. He shut down the mill last year. I'd like to get hold of that land, but only your grandmama has the money for that, and I don't think she'll put it up."

"Why not?"

Elinor laughed. "Why am I telling you all this? Do you care?"

"Yes, ma'am."

"No, you don't, darling. You don't know anything about it, and there's no reason for you to care one little bit." Elinor laughed, and held her daughter close.

When Sister Haskew moved away from Perdido in 1926 and took up residence first in Natchez and later in Chattanooga, she insisted on introducing herself to new acquaintances as Elvennia, her given name. By then she was thirty-five, two years older than her husband, and felt that it was high time she

110

was called by a name that was hers alone, and did not suggest—as the title "Sister" did—that her identity was subservient to a familial relationship. In her occasional visits to Perdido, however, nothing in the world could persuade Mary-Love Caskey from calling her daughter anything but Sister.

This was a minor irritation, however, and no more than was to have been expected from Mary-Love. Sister—or El, rather—was happy in her new life. She liked the sense of rootlessness after so many years of having had such strong bonds to Perdido, to the house in which she had been born, and to her mother. She liked making new friends who knew nothing of what she had been before her marriage to Early, who were wholly ignorant of sawmills and board feet, and didn't care about her family history. She wrote her mother twice a week, as Mary-Love had commanded, and on alternate weeks wrote to James and to Elinor. Sometimes, when Early was called away for a week or two on a job, Sister would pack her bag and take the train back to Perdido. On these occasions she would always begin to argue with her mother as soon as she walked in the door.

"Hello, Sister!" Mary-Love would cry. "We cain't tell you how much we have missed you!"

"Mama, everybody calls me El now."

"Oh, Sister, after all these years, you cain't expect me to change what I call my little girl..."

Mary-Love's little girl was now a woman of middle age, and Mary-Love herself was approaching old age, although she would never admit to such a thing.

"Sister," Mary-Love always wanted to know, "are you settled down yet? Have you got you a good cook?"

"Mama," said Sister, "I don't have a cook, I do all the cooking."

"Oh, Sister, is that man driving you into the ground and making you work all day long?"

"Mama, Early and I cain't afford to have a cook, so I do it myself."

"If you lived here, Ivey and I would be able to take care of you. You wouldn't have to lift a finger."

It was usually at this point that Sister, weary of making the old arguments, would simply say, "Mama, Early and I are never gone come back here, and the reason we aren't is that we don't want to live with you, because you drive us both crazy."

"I don't think you and Early are very happy in Chattanooga."

"We love it there!"

"I don't believe that you and Early would be happy anywhere."

"What do you mean?"

"If you and Early had been happy all these years away from me, then you would have had children. Now you're too old for that. And there must be a reason why you leave your husband and come to see me every three months, Sister."

"I come to see you, Mama, because every week you are on the telephone for half an hour saying, 'Sister, why don't you ever come home?'"

"If you loved your husband the way you should, you wouldn't be leaving him so often."

Mary-Love didn't approve of the independence exhibited by her daughter since her marriage to Early Haskew, and it was only a short step from that to disapproval of the man responsible for Sister's liberation. Because he wasn't around, it was convenient to attack him; and because Sister was his wife, she must be ever on the defensive. "I'm still not sure," Mary-Love said soon after Sister's arrival on a visit in late winter of 1936, "that Early Haskew was the right man for you, Sister."

"Who was?"

"Oh, somebody else. Somebody with a little education. A little polish."

"Early attended Auburn. Early's been to Europe. I never even got to go to college. And I never got taken to Europe, either."

"Does he still eat his peas off a knife blade?"

"He does! And he said one day he'd teach me how to do it too!"

"Does he eat that way in a restaurant?"

"Mama, we cain't afford to go out much."

Mary-Love shook her head and sighed. "I hate to see you grubbing for money, darling, when I have so much."

"Then give me some, and I won't have to grub."

"I cain't do that."

"Why not, Mama? It wouldn't hurt you to send me a little something now and then."

"Early would think I was interfering. And I would be."

"Early would endorse the checks as quick as they came, I believe. Mama, Early doesn't make a lot of money, but we get by. I don't have all the dresses I want, and there are times I don't have two dollars in my purse."

"I did not raise my little girl to live like that!"

"Then send us some money, Mama."

"I've been thinking," said Mary-Love.

"What?"

"I've been thinking we all ought to have a little vacation. Ought to go somewhere. We haven't been on a trip in a long time."

"If you want to spend a little money on me that way, that's all right, too. Where do you want us to go? And who is us?"

"Us is you and Miriam and me."

"Not Early?"

"Early's gone be working, I would suppose."

"Maybe not," said Sister, hoping to annoy her mother.

"I was thinking of going to Chicago in the summer."

"What for?"

"It's been preying on my mind—I would like to see the sights of Chicago before I die."

CHAPTER 38

Nectar

Sister knew that her husband had work contracted for the entire summer of 1936. Out of mischief, she said nothing of this to her mother until Mary-Love had consented to pay Early's way to Chicago. The day after Sister returned to Chattanooga, she called her mother and said, "Mama, Early cain't go with us after all. He's got a job with the Tennessee Valley Authority down around Sheffield, so I'm gone be free all summer. Anytime you want to go to Chicago is fine with me."

"Oh, Sister, I'm so happy!"

"So listen, you go on and make reservations, get a bunch of train tickets, and why don't you see if there's anybody else who'll go with us?"

"Who else would we want, darling?"

"Oh, James, maybe—and Danjo. Since you're going to take Miriam," Sister added, "maybe you should invite Frances too—"

"Sister, I will do no such thing! I cain't afford to

115

take the whole world. If Frances came along, I'd have to pay for everything for her, Oscar and Elinor cain't afford it. Besides, Frances might get sick again, and then we'd have to cancel the whole trip. I guess it's all right if Danjo comes—he's a sweet enough child and James will pay for him. It might be nice to have James, too, as long as we could hire on an extra baggage car on the way back for all that stuff he's bound to buy."

James agreed to go, but wanted to bring along not only Danjo but Queenie, and Queenie's children, too. Mary-Love grumbled at this, but ultimately acceded with enough bad grace to make James feel guilty for having pressed the matter. Mary-Love's difficulty was not with Queenie herself, but with Malcolm and Lucille. Mary-Love took some comfort in predicting, at least three times every day, that the entire trip would be ruined by that misbehaving pair. Frances was pointedly left out of all these plans. James offered to subsidize Frances's ticket and expenses, and said to Oscar and Elinor, "Lord, y'all, I'm gone have Danjo and Malcolm and Lucille to take care of, one more is not gone make a bit of difference. I'm just gone put 'em all on different-colored leashes..."

Oscar was hesitant to accept his uncle's offer. "Mama is taking Miriam, Mama ought to take Frances, too," he said. "Besides, James, you are paying for a whole raft of people to go up there. You're gone spend a fortune before you get halfway to Chicago."

"I don't mind one bit," James said. This was to be the first great family outing since the onset of the Depression, and James wanted it to include as many Caskeys as possible.

Oscar remained reluctant to let his daughter go, but Elinor finally interceded. She pointed out that for Frances to be left so conspicuously behind would be harder for the child to bear than all the slights and shabby treatment that she was certain to receive from Mary-Love and Miriam during the trip. After having being so long cooped up in the house, a total change would probably do the child a great deal of good. Frances was fourteen and her mother thought that she ought to see a little of the world.

So the party for the trip was set at ten: Mary-Love, Sister, Miriam, James, Danjo, Frances, Queenie, Malcolm, Lucille, and Ivey Sapp. Ivey was being taken along to act as shepherdess or beast-of-burden, as needed. Hotel rooms were secured, tickets on the L&N were bought at the Atmore station, quantities of cash in brand-new bills were obtained from the recently reestablished Perdido bank, wardrobes were augmented in Mobile and Montgomery, new luggage was purchased, insurance was taken out, cameras were loaded with film, and letters were sent off to friends whose homes were en route. The flurry of activity astonished Perdido. The Caskeys might have been setting out on an expedition to the South Pole, for all the planning that was going into this trip. They were to leave early on the morning of the first of July, arrive late the following night in Chicago, remain there ten days, and return to Perdido by way of St. Louis and New Orleans, with five days in each city.

By the end of June the children were frantic with excitement. Sometimes even cautious Frances and diffident Danjo had to be quelled. Sister spent several weeks in Perdido and assisted her mother in the preparations, which would have been a great burden to Mary-Love had Sister not been there to help, and to provide stimulating argument on every point.

The day before the party was to leave, Mary-Love announced that she intended to pay a visit to the big house next door to inspect the clothes and other necessities that had been packed for Frances. To Sister, she said, "I don't intend to allow Elinor's daughter to embarrass us with her paltry wardrobe."

"Well, Mama," Sister pointed out in reply, "even

117

if Elinor has packed Frances a suitcase full of rags, there's not enough time now to do anything about it."

Mary-Love went next door anyway, for the first time in more than five years, since her ineffectual plea for Elinor's intercession between her and her son.

"Miss Mary-Love, how are you?" said Elinor at the door, with no more surprise than if her mother-in-law had visited her the day before.

"I am just about driven into the ground, Elinor."

"Getting everybody ready, I suppose."

"That's right. In fact, I just dropped by to make sure that Frances was all set."

"I am packing her suitcases this very minute. I imagine that tonight I'll have to hit her over the head with a hammer to get her to go to sleep."

"All the children are excited," replied Mary-Love.

"Come on upstairs," said Elinor, "and see what I've packed for her. See if you can think of anything I've forgotten."

"Why, I'd be happy to do that," said Mary-Love, though she wondered how it was that Elinor was making her inspection trip so easy. As she followed her daughter-in-law into the house, Mary-Love peered into the darkened front parlor and remarked, "Looks like you have been changing things around."

"A little," replied Elinor. "Miss Mary-Love, it is burning hot outside. Let me get you some nectar."

"Oh, Elinor, I am so glad you suggested that! Last week I had a glass of your nectar from Manda Turk, and it was the best stuff I've ever tasted. Who gathers your blackberries for you?"

"I send Luvadia and Frances. Go on upstairs and I'll fix us both some. I'm a little thirsty too. Frances's room is right next to the sleeping porch. The suitcases are open on her bed."

"Where is Frances?"

"James drove her and Danjo out to Lake Pinchona. Frances loves to feed that alligator!"

"Frances is gone fall in one day and get eaten up," Mary-Love said calmly, as she mounted the stairs.

Elinor went into the kitchen and said to Zaddie, "You go upstairs and see if Miss Mary-Love needs any help. She's going to want to undo everything I've already done. I'm going to fix her some nectar." She took out the ice pick and began to chop ice.

"I *wish* Frances had some prettier things," said Mary-Love. She had gone through Frances's luggage, clucking disapproval of what had been packed, how Elinor had packed it, and even of the two small suitcases themselves. Now she was seated on the glider on the sleeping-porch and sipping her blackberry nectar. Elinor rocked gently in the swing and was thoughtfully stirring the overpoweringly sweet nectar that had been diluted with water and ice. "I wish you and Oscar would *let* me buy Frances some things," Mary-Love continued. "You two don't even let me see my grandchild anymore."

"Miss Mary-Love," said Elinor calmly, "that's just not so. Frances loves you to death—Frances loves everybody—but you won't let that child near you."

"Elinor! How could you say such a thing!"

"I can say it because it's perfectly true. Oscar and I don't spend much time at your house and you don't spend much time over here either, but we have never tried to discourage Frances from going over to see you. You're her grandmother, but you don't ever want to have anything to do with her. You and Miriam treat Frances as if she were dirt under your feet. She lay in that room sick as she could be for three years, and not once did you visit her. I was embarrassed to mention it when anybody asked me about it. It's hard for me to believe that you could be so deliberately cruel to your own granddaughter."

There was no rancor in Elinor's voice. She spoke

as if she stated obvious truths. The very baldness of Elinor's assertions wounded Mary-Love, who never looked at a thing directly, and now had no idea how to confront her daughter-in-law's unexpected forthrightness.

"Elinor! I am shocked. Aren't we taking Frances with us to Chicago tomorrow? Won't she and Miriam have the time of their lives?"

"Maybe," said Elinor. "That is, if Miriam will speak to Frances—and I'm not convinced that she will."

Mary-Love was growing even less certain how to respond to her daughter-in-law. Elinor's remarks had the substance but not the feel of an attack. Mary-Love temporized by glancing around the porch and commenting idly, "It's been so long since I've been here."

"That's your fault, Miss Mary-Love," said Elinor, cannily returning to the subject. "Oscar and I would never have turned you away if you had knocked on the door."

"I didn't feel welcome," said Mary-Love, abashed that her innocent-sounding tactic of delay had so quickly been turned against her. "This isn't my house anymore, you know."

Elinor didn't reply. Her smile was vague.

"You know," Mary-Love went on, "one day I sent Luvadia Sapp over here with the deed to this house. I signed it over to you and Oscar. Did that girl bring it, or did she lose it somewhere on the way?"

"Oh, she brought it. We've got the deed inside somewhere."

"I was expecting a thank you, I must say."

"Miss Mary-Love, Oscar and I bought this house."

"I *gave* it to you!"

"No, you're wrong," Elinor said with ostensible amiability. "It was *supposed* to have been our wedding present. But then we had to pay for it. We had to give you Miriam for it. Miriam was eight years

120

old before you finally turned over the deed. That kind of delay doesn't deserve a thank you."

Elinor's voice and tone continued soft and conversational, but Mary-Love was certain now that this attack had been long in the planning. She was little prepared to do battle when all her thought for months had been devoted to tomorrow's journey!

"I don't know why I'm sitting here listening to this," Mary-Love cried. "You're so hard! No wonder Frances is the way she is! No wonder Miriam doesn't want to play with her!"

"Frances, in case you hadn't noticed, is a thoroughly sweet child. She loves everybody, and everybody loves her. I wish I could say the same for Miriam. The way that child acts, I'm glad she lives with you and not with me."

"Miriam is worth ten of Frances!"

"You may think that, but it's still no excuse for you to treat Frances the way you do," said Elinor, remaining aggravatingly cool.

Mary-Love, in danger of becoming agitated, sought to turn the attack. "Elinor, why do you treat *me* the way you do?"

Elinor appeared to consider for a moment, and then replied: "Because of the way you treat Oscar. The way you treat your whole family, the way you've always treated them."

"I love every one of them! I love them to death! All I want in the world is for my family to love me."

"I know," said Elinor. "And you don't want them to love anyone else. You want to provide everybody with everything. You didn't want Oscar to marry me because you didn't want him to divide his love. The same with poor old Sister. You took Miriam away from us—"

"You let her go!"

"—and you raised her so that she loved you, and didn't give a single solitary thought to her own par-

121

ents. I remember back when Grace was little and was close to Zaddie, you tried to break that up, too."

"I don't remember anything of the sort!"

"You did it, though. Miss Mary-Love, it's the kind of thing you do without thinking. It comes natural to you. If you had had your way, James would have thrown Queenie Strickland and her children out of town the day they showed up."

"Queenie was no good—"

"You told James he was making a big mistake in taking in Danjo, but Danjo has made James very happy."

"One day that boy is going to turn—"

Elinor again paid no attention to Mary-Love. "And when the bank called in Oscar's loan, you wouldn't lend him the money to save him from bankruptcy. You *wanted* to see Oscar and me go under. You wanted us poor so that we would have to come begging."

"Oscar didn't go under. James lent him the money," Mary-Love protested.

"Oscar has never forgiven you. I don't imagine he ever will."

"You haven't either, have you, Elinor?"

"Miss Mary-Love, you don't like me because I took Oscar away from you. You haven't liked me since the day I showed up in Perdido. It can't make a whole lot of difference to you whether I forgive you or not."

"You're right," said Mary-Love, suddenly frank, almost without knowing it, letting her anger show and speaking her mind, "it doesn't. I've never expected anything from you except bitterness and reproach, Elinor. And it's all I've ever gotten. And this, I suppose, is your fond farewell with everybody about to go off to Chicago for a good time."

"Yes," replied Elinor, unperturbed. "Though you're not there yet."

"You've been biding your time, haven't you? You've been treasuring up your hostility, isn't that right?

You've been storing it up for five years, ever since Oscar asked me to lend him money he didn't even need!"

"I have been waiting..." Elinor admitted.

"I *wondered* when you were going to show your hand," snapped Mary-Love. "Since you showed up in this town during the flood, lounging in the Osceola and waiting for my boy to come along and rescue you and court you and marry you. Lying in wait for him like a lizard waiting for a green-bottle fly! And you got him. I couldn't stop you. But I *did* stop you from getting anything else, didn't I? For all your running-around, and all your little schemes and plans and biting, you've ended up with nothing at all."

"Nothing?" echoed Elinor.

"*Nothing.* What have you got? You've got this house, because I gave it to you. You've got a drawerful of promissory notes to James, and he's the only man in the world who would lend money to Oscar, who never had anything I didn't give him and never will. You've got a deed to a little land that's scattered around here and there, but it's all flood land and there aren't any roads on any of it and Tom De-Bordenave when he owned it never made a crying dime off it. And you've got a little girl, but she's a puny thing, and nothing at all compared to the one you gave away fifteen years ago. You've got a few friends in town, but they're the ones you stole from me. They're the ones I didn't want anymore. And you've got a husband who will insist on living next door to his mother forever. That's what you've got, Elinor, and let me tell you, it isn't much. Not by my standards."

"It seems to me," said Elinor, "that you've showed your hand too."

"No! I'm not the one who's fighting. I'm not the one who's always playing games. Because I'm on top. You try to blame me for beating you out of what's rightfully yours, but nobody beat you out, Elinor.

You just didn't have the courage to go out and get what you wanted."

"I've held back," Elinor returned.

Mary-Love laughed derisively. "I'd like to see you try to do something, Elinor. Just what do you think you *could* do, to get back at me for all the things you think I've done? What paltry little thing will you do now?"

"Miss Mary-Love, despite you and despite everything you've tried to do to keep Oscar down, I intend to make him rich. I intend to make him richer than you ever dreamed of being—that's what I intend to do."

Again Mary-Love laughed. "And how do you intend to do that? The last time you convinced him to do something, all he did was get himself in debt, and he's never gotten out of it. Are you gone persuade him to buy more land?"

"Yes. Henry Turk is going to sell his land—that's all that poor man's got left. He's got a tract of about fifty thousand acres in Escambia County. He came to see Oscar about it the other day."

"How much does he want for it?"

"Twenty dollars an acre."

"That's a hundred thousand dollars! Where's Oscar gone get that money?"

Elinor smiled. "I thought I'd take this opportunity to ask you to lend it to him."

Mary-Love's jaw dropped in her amazement. "Elinor, you are asking me to lend you one hundred thousand dollars so Oscar can buy a lot of worthless land?"

"It's not worthless. It's covered with pine."

"Lord God, what do we need more pine for? There's nobody buying it, Elinor. Or hadn't you heard there's a Depression going on?"

"We ought to have that land, Miss Mary-Love. Will you lend us the money?"

"No! Of course I'm not gone lend you the money!

You'd like to drive me to the poor house, is what you'd like to do, Elinor. Well, I'm not gone be driven anywhere, I'm not lending Oscar one penny. What has he been able to do with that land he bought from Tom DeBordenave? He hasn't even been able to keep up bank payments on it."

"Then your answer is no?"

"Of course it's no! Did you actually expect me to say yes?"

"No," admitted Elinor. "I just wanted to give you one more chance."

"One more chance for *what?*"

To this Elinor made no reply. She drank off the last of her nectar and put the glass on the table at the side of the swing.

"Miss Mary-Love," she replied, still unmoved, "think whatever you like about me. All I've said today is that I know what you're up to. I've always known. And when the time comes when you have the leisure to think things over, just remember that I gave you one last chance."

Mary-Love stood up from the glider and straightened her dress. "I'll tell you another thing, Elinor..."

"What?"

"You make the worst nectar I've ever had in my life. It tastes like you made it with water straight out of that stinking old river. The only reason I drank more than one sip was out of pure politeness."

The next morning a caravan of automobiles, filled with people and luggage, headed for the train station in Atmore. Florida Benquith drove Queenie, Queenie's children, and Ivey; Bray drove Mary-Love, Sister, and Miriam; and Oscar drove James, Danjo, and Frances. Everyone was jammed together and anxious to be off. Sister carried sheaves of tickets in her pocketbook. She had taken the responsibility of managing all the logistics of the excursion.

At the train station the Caskeys and all their luggage were lined up on the platform, waiting for the Hummingbird, which would take them as far as Montgomery. There they would change trains and be on their way directly to Chicago.

Mary-Love attempted to wheedle out of her son some small expression of affection: "Are you gone miss us?"

"You're taking away half the town, Mama."

"Say goodbye to me, Oscar!"

"Have a good time, Mama," said Oscar, perfunctorily kissing her on the cheek. She had not dared hope for more. She turned to thank Florida Benquith for her assistance, when she suddenly grew dizzy and grasped the back of a bench to keep from falling.

"Are you all right, Mary-Love?" asked Queenie.

Mary-Love looked up with an expression of pained surprise. "Suddenly I think I have got the worst headache I've ever had in all my life."

"Are you sick?" asked Miriam apprehensively. She had been looking forward to this trip, and wanted nothing to interfere with her pleasure in it.

"No, I've just got a headache. Sister, is everybody ready to go?"

"Yes, ma'am—"

Before Sister could continue, Mary-Love sank onto the bench and raised her hand to her rapidly paling face.

"I don't know what's wrong with me," she gasped.

The adults gathered around her. Malcolm and Lucille stood to one side and drew on sullen faces in preparation for some great disappointment. Frances and Miriam looked toward their grandmother with some misgiving. She looked very ill.

Ivey moved forward and felt Mary-Love's forehead. Already her hair lay in damp waves over her prickled scalp.

"Miss Mary-Love, you hot?"

"Ivey," she whispered, "I'm just burning up!"

Ivey turned to the others and said, "She got a bad

126

fever. She ought to be at home in bed right this very minute. Y'all back off some." She took a kerchief from her pocketbook and handed it to Miriam. "Go get this wet."

Miriam hurried off to the ladies' room. The rest of them talked in low voices, glancing at Mary-Love. Her head lolled on her shoulders as Ivey sat beside her, unbuttoning her blouse, and wiping the perspiration from her forehead.

"She's real sick," said Florida. As the wife of a doctor, her opinion carried some weight.

"I know," said James, "but will she be all right?"

"Once she gets home, probably," replied Florida. "Leo ought to look at her. I never saw anybody get so sick so fast."

There was a moment of uncomfortable silence, then Sister's teeth went *clack-clack* and she said, "All right, then, I'll say it."

"Say what?" asked James weakly.

"What are we gone do? Are we gone go back to Perdido and sit around for five more years before we ever get out of town again?"

"Mary-Love looks so bad!" said James.

"Florida and I will take care of Mama," said Oscar. "The rest of y'all ought to get on that train. We got to think of the children. They'll be so disappointed if y'all turned around now."

"I know," sighed James. "But it just doesn't seem right to leave like this."

"Probably she would *want* you all to go on and have a good time," suggested Florida. "I don't think she would want to ruin everything for everybody."

Sister laughed. "Florida, don't you know Mama better than that? Nothing would make her well sooner than to know that we had canceled the entire trip because of her."

"Sister!" cried James.

"Well, I'm sorry, but that's the truth," said Sister, "but we have been planning this for months, and it's the first real chance I've had to go anywhere or do anything since I got married. I don't intend to give it all up just because Mama comes down with a summer cold."

"It looks worse than that," Queenie said. "But I agree with Sister, James. The children are excited— we're *all* excited. The tickets are paid for, the hotel reservations have all been made. And what would we say in Perdido, that all ten of us turned right around and came back when we weren't fifty miles out of town, just because Mary-Love came down with a little headache and temperature?"

"I suppose you're right," said James.

"Of course they're right," said Oscar energetically. "We'll put Mama in the back seat of the Packard and have her home in bed before y'all get to Greenville. As soon as she's well, we'll pack her up and send her on to meet you."

"Then it's settled," said Sister quickly. This seemed the solution that would do the least damage to their original plans, and she wanted to make it firm before James, in his charity to Mary-Love, could change anyone's mind. "Somebody should go speak to the children and tell them what's been decided."

Mary-Love Caskey sat and moaned and sweated profusely on the hard wooden bench in the stifling Atmore station. She could not speak an articulate word. Beside her, Ivey Sapp mopped her brow, squeezed her hands, and whispered, "Miss Mary-Love, Miss Mary-Love, what you been eating? What you been drinking? D'you get hold of something that wasn't good for you? You been drinking down some bad water?"

CHAPTER 39

The Closet Door Opens

Elinor was sitting on her front porch when Bray drove up. As if she had known that Mary-Love lay feverish across the back seat of the car, she stood up and walked out to the street and peered in. "Bray," she said, "I've got the front room all ready for her."

"Miss El'nor," said Bray, puzzled, "did Mr. Oscar call you on the telephone to say we was coming?"

Elinor, appearing preoccupied, did not answer.

Oscar had driven up right behind Bray and had heard what his wife had said. "Elinor," he said, "you sure you want this responsibility? I was thinking we maybe should put her in the hospital."

"Did Ivey look at her?"

Bray nodded. "Ivey say she ought to be at home in her own bed."

"That's not the hospital," Elinor pointed out. "Zaddie and I will take perfectly good care of her."

Bray lifted Mary-Love out of the car and quickly carried her into Elinor's house, up the stairs and down the corridor, placing her on the bed in the front room.

Elinor followed them in, calling Zaddie up.

"All of you go away, now," said Elinor, closing the door of the room against them. "Zaddie and I are going to change her clothes and give her a sponge bath. She'll be cooler and more comfortable then. Oscar, you better call Leo Benquith and get him over here."

Everyone did as they were told. Dr. Benquith arrived to find Mary-Love looking very weak and very ill, propped up on the pillows in the front room. She appeared now, however, to have some awareness of where she was. She was so little her old self that she did not even object to being placed in the care of her daughter-in-law. Elinor and Zaddie stood at the foot of the bed as Leo Benquith examined her.

"It's a fever," he said with a shrug. "Just what everybody said it was. And, Elinor, you did exactly the right thing. Miz Caskey," he said, addressing Mary-Love—rather loudly, as if deafness were also her infirmity, "Elinor's gone take good care of you till you get well."

Mary-Love's eyes closed and she sighed heavily.

That evening at supper, Oscar said to Elinor, "You sure we shouldn't put Mama in the hospital?"

"You heard what Leo Benquith said," replied Elinor. "I know what to do—and Leo will drop by every afternoon. Miss Mary-Love would hate the hospital—all those strangers. And, Oscar, when they start calling from Chicago, you tell them she's doing just fine, but doesn't want to talk on the telephone. If they think she's still sick, they'll all pack up and head right back. Your Mama has this family trained."

"Don't you think people *should* be here?"

"I do not. I think they'd only disturb her. I'm going to shoo away all her visitors until she can get well. By the time they all get back, your mama will be up

130

and complaining how they all left her high and dry. She's never going to let them hear the end of it."

Mary-Love was nursed by her daughter-in-law. Elinor sat with her in the front room all day long. All visitors were stopped at the door downstairs by an unbribable, unmovable Zaddie. Only Leo Benquith was allowed inside the house, and he came once a day, right after the noontime meal. He examined Mary-Love in Elinor's presence, went downstairs, and always accepted a glass of iced tea from Zaddie who was waiting for him with it. He sat out on the front porch and told Oscar what he thought.

What he thought was not very encouraging.

"Oscar," said Leo, "I don't know what's wrong with your mama. She has some sort of fever, and she cain't seem to get rid of it. She's gone have to lie real still up there for some time to come."

"Maybe we should take her to Pensacola to Sacred Heart..." Oscar suggested tentatively.

"Well," said Leo. "I wouldn't recommend it. I would let her keep to her bed. I would let Elinor stay right there by her all the time. Here she can have the food and drink that she's used to. That's what I would do."

"Leo, what is it she's *got*, anyway?"

"Like I said, it's some kind of fever. Like a swamp fever. Sort of like malaria—but of course it's not malaria. Honest to God, Oscar, I don't know what it is. Your mama been out fishing lately?"

"It's hard to imagine Mama fishing. Why you ask something like that?"

"'Cause I remember a long time ago an old colored man—don't even remember his name—came down with the same thing, or same thing near as I can make out. He was one of Pa's cases, I was just ittybitty, but I remember, 'cause I was going around with Pa in those days. That old colored man was a fisherman, used to fish on the Perdido a few miles up above here, I guess."

"That was before my time, 'cause I don't remember him. But he had the same thing?"

"I think it was. Said he fell in the water, swallowed some, and nearly drowned. Came back home and crawled into bed."

"Great God in the morning, Leo! If you could catch something out of Perdido water, don't you think we'd all be dead by now? Elinor, especially. She swims in that old river all the time. Always has. And she hasn't been sick a day since we were married in James's living room. What happened to that old colored man anyway?"

"Oh, Oscar, that was so long ago! That old man's been dead twenty-five years!"

"What'd he die of, though?" Leo Benquith looked closely at Oscar, but didn't answer. "That old colored man died of the fever he caught in Perdido water, isn't that right?" Oscar shook his head ruefully. "Leo, I'm sorry. It's not that I don't think you're the best doctor in three counties, it's just that lately Mama and I haven't been getting along so well."

"So Florida told me."

"And if anything happened to her right now, I think I'd just die! Listen, Leo, you think if I went up there and apologized, Mama would hear me and understand what I was saying?"

"She might."

"Would it be all right to do that?"

"As long as you don't badger her into answering you, 'cause I'm not so sure she can. Oscar, I tell you what. You wait awhile, let her get over the excitement of my being here this afternoon, then go up and ask Elinor if it's all right. She'll know."

"Elinor's a good nurse for Mama!" Oscar exclaimed with pride.

"She sure is," agreed Leo. "I think Elinor knows as much about Mary-Love's illness as I do."

132

Accordingly, an hour later, after he had drunk two more glasses of iced tea and walked around the house a couple of times and poked a stick into the kudzu at the base of the levee looking for stray snakes and called for Zaddie to let him in the back way, Oscar went upstairs and knocked on the door of the front room.

Elinor opened the door softly and stepped out into the hallway.

"How's Mama?"

"She's the same."

"Elinor, can I speak to her?"

"About what?"

"About...things," he said vaguely and uneasily.

"Are you gone yell at her?"

"No, of course not! I'm gone ask her to forgive me."

"Forgive you for what?"

"For not coming to see her for the past five years."

"Oscar, that was Mary-Love's fault. That wasn't yours."

"I know, but I shouldn't have done it anyway. Mama's always been that way, and I knew it. Maybe if I said, 'Mama, will you forgive me?' it'd make her feel better. You think?"

Elinor paused and considered. At last she stood aside and said, "All right, Oscar. Go on in. But keep your voice down. And don't keep asking her to say yes and no and shake her head and kiss you."

"I won't. But will she hear me? Will she understand what I'm saying?"

"That I don't know. Oscar, I'm going to speak to Zaddie for a few minutes and then I'm coming right back up and throw you out. So you'd better get to it."

Elinor went quietly down the hallway toward the stairs as Oscar hesitantly entered the front room.

The room was dark and airless, though outside the sun shone brightly and a stiff breeze from the

Gulf kept the afternoon heat at bay. Across the windows the shades had been pulled, the venetian blinds closed, and the lined draperies drawn. A thin line of dim light along the baseboard below the windows was the only indication that it was not black night outside. The room was overwhelmed with the unmistakable odor of illness, as if the sickness had infected the bedclothes, the furniture, and the very walls and floor of the room. On a table laden with medicines was an oscillating fan. Its labored turning was a result of mechanical difficulty, but it almost seemed to Oscar that its problems might have been caused by the density of the air it had to reckon with. An extra carpet had been put down on the floor; cushions had been put on all the chairs, and cloths had been laid over every surface to guard against obtrusive noise. A single low-watted bulb shone dimly behind a shade of crimson silk. Oscar looked about and no longer wondered that his daughter had been afraid to sleep in this room. The walls were dark green, but they seemed no brighter than the black cast-iron chandelier suspended near the middle of the ceiling. He had rarely been in this room. With the door closed, the light shut out, and all outside sound muffled, it didn't seem like a part of the house at all.

In the same way, his mother, lying in the bed, seemed no longer a part of his life. She was not the woman who figured in his memory and thought. Mary-Love lay unmoving, breathing stertorously, in a thick linen nightdress, propped up on pillows. The sheets, spread, and coverlet had been impeccably arranged; they covered Mary-Love almost up to her neck. Her hands, white and frail, lay atop the folded-back sheet.

Mary-Love's eyes were open, but they were not focused on her son. Experimentally, he moved a few feet to the left. Her eyes did not follow him. Oscar placed himself in her line of vision.

134

"Mama?" he said.

He listened and wondered if he did not detect a slight momentary alteration of her breath. It was difficult to tell over the distracting noise of the fan.

"Mama, I came to visit you for a minute."

He moved to the table and turned the fan off. For the first time he detected the unsettling raspiness in his mother's breathing.

Back at bedside, he assured her, "I'll turn it back on in a minute. I just wanted to make sure you heard what I was going to say."

He paused, waiting for some indication that she had heard, or that she assented to his continuing. None came, but Oscar felt that he had to proceed.

"Mama, I'm real sorry you're sick. The only good thing about your being sick is that you're letting Elinor and me take care of you. You know what that shows, don't you? It shows nobody's upset anymore. Elinor wouldn't do everything she's doing for you if she were still mad at you, would she? She wouldn't spend all day up here every day. She wouldn't sleep in here at night. Mama, I just want you to know that I'm not mad anymore either. I'm not even thinking about the things that made me mad. I just want you to get well. By the time everybody comes back from Chicago, I want you back in your own house, fussing. I want you to get mad because everybody went away and left you here by yourself. But I tell you something, I'm glad they did, because it means Elinor and I have got the chance to prove how much we really do love you. That's what I wanted to make sure you heard me say. Just because I'm not being your nurse doesn't mean I don't care, because I do. I just wouldn't know what to do in here. See, I cain't even look at you and make sure you're hearing what I'm saying. I wouldn't know what medicine was what, and that's why Elinor is doing all this and not me. Elinor is being better than I thought she could be, Mama. Now, doesn't it make you want to cry that you two

135

have not been getting along all these years? You know what? Elinor and I have been married sixteen years now, isn't that something? I remember the first time—"

At that moment, Elinor opened the door of the room, and said, "Oscar, that's enough for right now. It's time for your mama's medicine. Turn the fan back on."

He did so. "Do you think she heard me?" he asked. "I said some things I wanted to make sure she heard."

Elinor turned her gaze to the woman in the bed. "I'm sure she heard every word." From a tray beside the fan, she took up a bottle of reddish liquid, unscrewed the cap, and poured out a dose into an old silver soupspoon.

"Can you tell for sure?" he persisted anxiously.

"Yes. Oscar, it's time you got back to the mill. You can speak to Mary-Love later." She went around the bed with the medicine.

"Is that Leo's prescription?"

With one hand she pressed Mary-Love's cheeks sharply together, so that her mouth involuntarily opened. Oscar watched as Elinor poured the liquid in, then rapped upward Mary-Love's chin so that her mouth clapped shut with a clack of teeth.

"No," replied Elinor, standing up straight, "this is mine."

Oscar stood at the door and opened it softly. "Elinor, I'll be back at five." He looked once more at his mother in the bed. Mary-Love's eyes now seemed to stare back at him. In them Oscar saw what he thought was fear. "Mama," he said, "Elinor's gone take good care of you."

He slipped out and closed the door quickly behind him. He did not see his mother's lips struggle to form three syllables.

"Per-di-do," Mary-Love whispered.

Elinor looked at her mother-in-law and turned the

136

fan on high. Mary-Love's rasping breath could not be heard.

Elinor sat down in the rocker at the foot of the bed and opened a magazine on her lap.

Mary-Love's fingers weakly twisted the hem of the sheet. Her moving lips formed the words, "I'm drowning..."

Feebleness, inconsequence, immobility, dependence—things Mary-Love Caskey had never known before had suddenly crowded in upon her. She remembered getting sick in the Atmore station, and she remembered when she first opened her eyes in the front room. She knew where she was from the hand-painted flowers on the footboard of the bed; she had picked the suite out in Mobile. It was the first furniture she had purchased for her son's house.

Her limbs were without sensation and very cold at the same time. Her head burned. She seemed always to be waking up, though she never had to open her eyes. She could never remember falling asleep. She wished she could dream. As it was, nothing held her mind but her cold limbs, her burning brow, and the profile of Elinor Caskey, rocking in a chair at the foot of the bed. Zaddie appeared sometimes, and the young black woman's voice seemed distant as she spoke to Elinor. It was as if Mary-Love heard it from the house next door, as if it were a voice caught in her sleep.

Elinor's voice, in contrast, always sounded close and clear, as if the words had been whispered directly into Mary-Love's ear in the dark.

She was never hungry, and she never remembered having eaten anything. The only thing she remembered was Elinor's fingers pressing her cheeks, so that the red liquid from the unmarked medicine bottle could be poured between her opened lips. Hours later, she'd feel the grit it left behind, pressing against her gums and her teeth. She wondered at Leo Benquith's prescribing it. Afterward, she always felt worse and weaker.

As the days progressed—Mary-Love supposed they were days, but reckoned them only by the difference in outfits Zaddie wore when she came into the room with the trays bearing Elinor's meals—Mary-Love lost more and more sensation in her body. Her limbs were no longer cold, but the sheets, the spread, and the coverlet were leaden upon her. Her hands rested free, but the very air of the room seemed weighted; it seemed to press down against her until she could not move at all. She felt the perspiration that gathered upon her brow, which sometimes dripped into her eyes and stung. She welcomed that sting, for it was the only sensation left to her.

Otherwise, she was overwhelmed with the sense that she was filling up with liquid, as if her body were only some stretching skin into which day by day Elinor poured that noxious red liquid. It wasn't sweet, but it reminded her of the blackberry nectar she had been served the day before she fell ill. Her legs and belly were already so heavy that they seemed to sink deep into the bed. She was certain that she would never be able to move them again. A soup-spoon of that medicine seemed to fill her body with gallons of liquid! She grew heavier and heavier. It was filling her lungs, leaving little room for her to bring in air. Her breath grew shallow and quick, and she felt that she was beginning to drown. Her brain held an involuntary image of floating slowly down the Perdido, her body lying just below the surface, with only her mouth, eyes, and nose protruding into the air. The rest of her was submerged in the river. If she struggled, she would certainly drown in that dry, airless front bedroom of Oscar's house. Even if the draperies were drawn back, the venetian blinds opened, and the shades lifted, Mary-Love would have seen only the levee, not the Perdido behind it, the

Perdido daily spooned between her lips by her daughter-in-law.

Mary-Love was certain that that unmarked bottle held Perdido water. She now recognized the taste. She knew the texture of the red clay granules that were left behind on her tongue when she swallowed. She could smell it whenever the bottle was unscrewed. Yet she couldn't prevent her lips from parting when Elinor squeezed her cheeks, and couldn't help but swallow when Elinor jarred her mouth shut again.

Elinor was tireless. Elinor never left her.

Mary-Love prayed to be alone; she prayed to die in peace. She prayed to be able to sleep dreamlessly forever. She prayed for some death other than that which her daughter-in-law was preparing for her. When she realized that none of these prayers was to be answered, she beseeched God only that her doom not be prolonged.

Elinor sat at the foot of Mary-Love's bed and rocked. She leafed quietly through stacks of magazines and took trays from Zaddie at the door. She stood by reporting to Leo Benquith, and when he was gone, she poured whole currents of Perdido river water down her mother-in-law's throat.

Once only did Mary-Love Caskey come to consciousness and find her daughter-in-law absent from the room. Her eyes, as usual, were already open. The sense of waking had not come to her, only the realization that previously she had been asleep. She hadn't the power to move her eyes in their sockets. She could only stare directly before her. Elinor was not in her chair. By some subtle means she couldn't precisely figure out, Mary-Love knew that Elinor was not in the room—and she also knew that it was night.

She drew an extra breath—a tiny sniff that wouldn't have been noticed even by someone leaning over her—in order to feel to what extent her lungs had filled with water.

Mary-Love's heart contracted. She had only an inch of space remaining in her lungs. Only an inch of breath to sustain her. She was heavy, filled with Perdido water, and the water was rising.

Lungs don't work that way, some voice belonging to the old Mary-Love told her sternly. Bodies don't fill with water like cauterized skins. Women don't drown in their beds.

Mary-Love didn't want to panic. If she panicked, she'd gasp for breath. If she gasped for breath, the water would move and slosh, and she'd die sputtering. She hadn't any hope except to cling to life. She wanted to stave off that doom for which she had so recently prayed.

She continued by force only to breathe her shallow, almost imperceptible breaths.

The front room darkened, as if she had closed her eyes, yet Mary-Love knew her eyes were open. She could not know how long it remained so. She felt, however, that she never lost consciousness.

Light came suddenly, but it wasn't morning light. It wasn't lamplight. It wasn't light from the opened door to the corridor. It was merely a pale bluish-white glow, outlining the closet door to the right of the fireplace.

Mary-Love made an effort to focus her eyes upon it. That was as much as she could do.

The closet door was slowly opening.

A little boy stood inside, and he was looking about himself in apparent confusion. Like Mary-Love, he also seemed not to have awakened, but to have found himself in a state of consciousness that had not existed before. He lifted his hand before his face and stared at it. He peered cautiously out into the darkened room. Though Mary-Love thought that she knew him, she could not think clearly enough to identify him. Was he one of hers? Was he Queenie's boy?

The child stepped out of the closet and into the room. The bluish-white light faded behind him. The room was dark again.

Though the fan was off, Mary-Love heard nothing but her own shallow breathing.

Now that she could no longer see him, the boy's name came to her suddenly. *John Robert De-Bordenave.*

More than his name came into her memory.

John Robert had disappeared twelve years before. He had drowned in the Perdido during the final stage of the levee construction, but now appearing so briefly in the light of the opened closet door, he was no older than on the last day that Mary-Love had seen him.

Has Elinor kept that boy locked up in there?

She heard a stray footfall then, though it was infinitely soft against the carpet.

Propped on her pillows, hands clasped neatly outside the regimented covers, Mary-Love might have been arranged for a visit from five governors and a member of the Cabinet. In the darkness, she could see nothing.

Then, there was a tug on the sheet, the hem of which was folded beneath her hands. Powerless to resist, her hands slipped apart.

Mary-Love saw nothing, but by a creek of springs, and a shifting of the mattress, she knew that John Robert DeBordenave was crawling beside her into the bed.

CHAPTER 40

The Wreath

The Caskeys had a wonderful time in Chicago, St. Louis, and New Orleans. The adults were as full of wonder and enjoyed themselves as much as the children. Only Miriam seemed out of sorts. She missed her grandmother sorely, or rather she missed her grandmother's never-yielding championship of her superiority to other children. Without Mary-Love, Miriam was just another little girl, with no special privileges above those accorded to Frances and Queenie's children.

Every day, James telephoned Oscar to ask how Mary-Love was getting along. Every day, Oscar said that she was improving, though still unable to write, still unwilling to get out of bed and come to the telephone. He did not say that there was a stack of postcards from Chicago, St. Louis, and New Orleans sitting on the hall table downstairs, unadmired and unread. He did not say that since James had left, Mary-Love Caskey had not spoken a single intelligible word to him, or evinced the slightest interest or curiosity about anything whatsoever, and that the front room, which had first smelled of sickness, had now begun to smell of something stronger.

James Caskey may have heard some of this in Oscar's tone and in Oscar's evasions. But no one else in the party suspected anything except that Mary-Love would be dreadfully angry with them all when they got home. On the last leg of the journey, the five-hour ride from New Orleans to Atmore, they all sat quietly in their compartments. Most of the talk was of facing Mary-Love on their return. The consensus was that Mary-Love would never forgive them for leaving her at home and going off and having a good time on their own.

"Lord," sighed James, "I know she's gone come down hard. That's why we haven't heard a single word from her. She's saving up."

"She's gone say," said Sister, "'I got well in two days flat, but y'all wouldn't wait, y'all just went on without me.'"

"She's gone say," said Queenie, "'I paid for this trip, and I want y'all to know that I didn't get one moment's pleasure out of it. Don't anybody ever ask me again, "Miss Mary-Love, can we go somewhere?" 'cause I'm not paying for anybody to go anywhere ever again!'"

They laughed at the predictability of her reaction at the same time that they dreaded her displeasure.

A few miles before the termination of the journey, the weary party began to gather in the train's narrow corridor. They would have very little time to get off the train, and the group was loaded down with what they had taken with them as well as what they had picked up along the way. All the Caskeys stood in a long line with Ivey foremost, and James and Sister in the rear. Queenie and the children were in the middle. Everyone stared out the window, watching for the first exciting glimpse of a familiar landmark or person.

As the train began to slow, the children grew restive until Danjo pointed and cried out, "I see Bray!"

"There's Miz Benquith!" cried Lucille.

"Daddy!" whispered Frances.

At the very end of the line, Sister peered through the open door of the compartment and out the window on the opposite side of the car. In the parking lot of the station she saw Oscar's automobile, Florida Benquith's car, and the Packard. Wired to the grille of the Packard was a black wreath.

As the train pulled into the station the children covered their ears at the shrill whistle.

But it wasn't a whistle, it was Sister's high-pitched wail of anguish, rising behind them, pushing them all out of the corridor, down the metal steps, and into the burning Alabama sun. As they stood bewildered on the platform before the station with Sister still wailing behind them, Bray and Oscar stepped forward with bands of mourning crape around their arms.

A black wreath had been hung on the door of each of the Caskey houses and over the gate of the Caskey mill. Mary-Love lay in a great white wicker casket, which resembled nothing so much as a oversized bassinet lined with a cushion of deep purple satin.

After Elinor had discovered the body the previous morning, Mary-Love had been taken away by the undertaker and brought back in only a few hours, clad in the dress she had worn the previous Easter. The furniture had been moved around in Elinor's front parlor and the casket placed beneath the stained-glass windows. In the colored light, the undertaker explained, the unavoidable alterations in skin color would be less noticeable. Mounds of lilies and heavily scented gardenias in tubs covered with gold foil surrounded the casket. They masked the disagreeable odor of corruption, which came quickly to the dead in an Alabama July.

When Bray and Oscar and Florida Benquith had gone off to fetch the unsuspecting Caskeys from the Atmore station, the casual Perdido mourners were quietly ushered out of the house by Elinor, and the wreath was temporarily removed from the door to discourage others. Elinor sat in the parlor, quietly leafing through magazines, just as she had done when Mary-Love had lain, dying, in the room directly above this; Zaddie and Roxie were in the kitchen preparing food. A great deal of food had been brought by the townspeople, for nothing—everyone knew—makes one hungrier than grief.

At last Elinor heard the approach of the three automobiles. She went out onto the porch and stood silently.

Frances jumped out of the first car, and, weeping bitterly, ran toward her mother.

All the others emerged more slowly. They struggled with luggage and packages, talked in low voices, and wouldn't look at the house. No one seemed to know what to do first.

"Leave your things there," said Elinor in a low voice heard by everyone. "And come inside."

The family trooped silently onto the porch. Florida Benquith, having done her part, drove slowly away, as quietly as possible.

"Where'd you put her, Elinor?" asked James.

"In the front parlor."

Zaddie stood just inside the screen door. She pulled it open and stood back, nodding to everyone who came in. She spoke in a low voice. "How you, Miss Queenie? Hey, Danjo, you have a good time at Chicken-in-the-car-and-the-car-won't-go-Chicago?"

At last, only Elinor and her estranged daughter Miriam were left on the porch. The sixteen-year-old looked up at her mother, and said, "Why is Grandmama over here?"

146

"Because we couldn't leave her next door. There was no one to sit up with her. There was no one to receive visitors. And because she died in this house."

"She hated it over here," remarked Miriam as she went inside to survey the remains of her dead grandmother.

"She never looked prettier," was the general comment, but the actual thought was that Mary-Love had never looked worse. Her face was wasted, drawn tight over the bones in some places, slack in others. Her folded hands seemed twisted in frustration. She looked anything but sleeping, anything but natural.

"Can she hear us?" Danjo whispered. James shook his head.

Miriam stood at the end of the coffin and peered into it for half a minute or so. Her eyes were dry. "Where are her rings?" she asked at last.

That night, Sister sat up with the body, joined in the first part of the night by James, then later by Oscar. In that room, under those circumstances, the Caskeys seemed all at once to have grown old. It had been a long time since any important member of the family had died. James and Mary-Love had been of an exact age, and James's sixty-six years now made him appear an old man—to his family as well as to himself. Oscar was forty-one, and in the presence of his mother's corpse, he looked every year of it. Sister was three years older, and that difference now appeared even greater. In the darkest hours, the brother and sister sat on the couch that faced the casket and talked about everything in the world but their mother. At last, as dawn approached and the first light glowed in through the panes of the colored glass over the casket, Sister said, "She wasn't old. Sixty-six isn't old."

"She was very sick. Sister, you didn't see her in that room up there."

"What was *wrong* with her?"

147

"We don't know. After Bray and I brought her back here from Atmore, she didn't speak a single word to anybody. And she wasn't left alone for a minute."

"She must have been," Sister pointed out. "Nobody was with her when she died."

"Elinor went downstairs for two seconds, and when she came back, Mama was gone."

"As long as there wasn't any pain..."

"Sister, I wish I could say for sure that there wasn't, but I don't know. Maybe I'm just not used to being around the mortally ill, but I never saw anything like it."

"Like what?"

"Like what happened in that front room up there."

"What do you mean? What happened?"

"Nothing happened. That's what I mean. She was in that room all the while you were gone. She didn't move, she didn't speak, she didn't close her eyes. Either Elinor or Zaddie was with her all the time. Elinor slept on a rollaway at the foot of the bed. I just don't know whether Mama was in pain or not. All I know is that Elinor took care of her like she was her own mama, and had loved her every day of her life. If Mama had lived, I suppose they would gone back to their old ways, but while Mama was sick, Elinor was always there. That must have made Mama feel good, if she knew it..."

"I'm not so sure about that, Oscar."

As the sun rose over the pecan orchard opposite the house, the stained-glass windows were suddenly flooded with bright light. The wicker casket sprang to prominence before them, and Mary-Love's ringless fingers were stained a bright blue.

Visitors began arriving at seven-thirty that morning for a last respectful view of the corpse. An endless round of breakfasts and an inexhaustible supply of coffee were set in the dining room by Zaddie, Ivey, and Roxie.

148

The funeral service was held in the parlor with only the family present. Early Haskew had been alerted the morning of Mary-Love's death, and he arrived with only an hour to spare. Grace couldn't be found because she was off on some sort of expedition to the Great Smoky Mountains National Park with her friend who taught English literature.

While the funeral in the parlor was private, the service at the cemetery was open, and almost the entire town showed up. The mill had been closed for the day, and all the workers wandered about at a distance among the other graves, reading epitaphs aloud, toeing rocks out of the sandy earth, and slapping their thighs with the brims of their hats. Mary-Love's coffin was lowered into the earth next to Genevieve's. James, Sister, and Queenie wept.

After the graveside service, all the citizens of Perdido seemed to disperse themselves for the remainder of the afternoon. Little business was done. The Caskeys retired to their separate houses and grieved alone.

Elinor and Oscar had a houseful of food. Zaddie and Bray made a number of trips that quiet afternoon, delivering casseroles and hams and messes of peas and the like to the other Caskeys, who for certain didn't yet feel like cooking anything.

Elinor, Oscar, and Frances sat on the porch upstairs. The day had turned even hotter than usual, and unpleasantly damp. Even the kudzu on the levee appeared to wilt beneath the atmospheric oppression. The creaking chains of the swing seemed muted, and downstairs Zaddie was working barefoot.

"Are you sad?" Oscar asked his daughter.

Frances nodded. She sat on the swing beside her mother, holding Elinor's hand.

"It was a shock, wasn't it?"

Frances nodded again.

"Elinor," remarked Oscar, "Sister asked me this

149

morning why we didn't tell them all to come home when Mary-Love was so sick."

"You know why we didn't, Oscar."

"Why?"

"Because it wouldn't have done any good to have everybody here. In fact, it would have done your mama harm. All those people traipsing in and out all day. She would never have gotten a minute's rest."

"But she died anyway," Frances pointed out. "And nobody got to see her."

"Frances is right," said her father. "When everybody got back, there was Mama in her casket. I don't blame them for feeling as bad as they do. James said it's horrible to think that while they were all having such a good time in Chicago and St. Louis and New Orleans, Mama was lying in the front room, suffering and dying, and they didn't know a thing about it."

"Oscar, that's the point. Even if they had known anything, they couldn't have helped."

"Mama would have wanted everybody at home."

"Yes!" said Frances.

"Well," said Elinor, "your mama wasn't running the show. I was."

Oscar said nothing more, but continued to fan himself diligently with a paper fan bearing an advertisement for the undertaker. After a bit he stood up, went over to the edge of the porch and looked out at his mother's house. He turned, appeared about to say something, then changed his mind and remarked suddenly, "Did you notice that Early was chewing tobacco?"

"At the funeral?"

"Yes!" cried Frances. "Miriam saw him spit into a camellia bush, and after that she wouldn't speak to him. She said he was too country for words."

"How long do you suppose Early's gone stay around?" asked Oscar.

"How should I know?" Elinor said.

"You might have spoken to him."

"Well, I didn't," said Elinor. "What difference does it make?"

"Because Sister will probably go back with him, that's why."

"And?"

"And then what becomes of Miriam?"

"Miriam," said Elinor definitely, "comes home to us."

"Home?" echoed Oscar. "Miriam's never lived here. I don't imagine she's stepped foot in this house more than six times in her entire life."

"You think she really might move over here?" asked Frances with suppressed excitement.

"Where else would she go?" returned Elinor. "In a day or so I'll send Zaddie over to pack up her clothes."

"Mama," said Frances hesitantly, "are you gone give Miriam my room?"

"Of course not! We'll put Miriam in the front room."

"She cain't sleep in there!" cried Oscar.

"Why not?"

"Mama died in there! Mama died in that bed!"

"Well, Oscar, that's not going to hurt Miriam. Miss Mary-Love herself slept for twenty years in that bed your daddy died in. In fact, she probably slept in it the very night your daddy died, didn't she?"

Oscar nodded.

"I don't think Miriam will be scared," said Frances quietly. "If she is, she can sleep with me."

Elinor smiled at her daughter. "Aren't you a little old to be sharing your bed?"

"Was Miriam good to you on your trip?" Oscar asked.

"Yes, sir..." replied Frances slowly.

"Really and truly?" her mother prompted.

"Well, she was a little short with me now and then,

151

but I didn't care. She was probably just worried about Grandmama."

Oscar and Elinor exchanged glances.

"Miriam," said Miriam's father, "may need a little talking to."

"Miriam wants to know where Grandmama's rings are, Mama."

"She said something about that to you?"

"At the funeral."

"What did you say?"

Frances hesitated.

"Frances, what did Miriam say about the rings?"

"She said they were hers and that you stole them. She said Grandmama gave them to her for her safety-deposit box in Mobile."

Elinor said nothing, but her expression was hard.

"Elinor, Miriam's bound to be upset. You know how she loved Mama. Lord, she lived with Mama all her life, she—"

"It's all right, Oscar. I'm not upset. One way or another, Miriam and I will be able to work things out."

CHAPTER 41

Mary-Love's Heir

With Mary-Love dead, the complexion of the Caskey family was greatly altered. Mary-Love had been its head, its guiding force, its principal source of rebuke, and the measure by which all its achievements, delights, and unhappinesses were judged. She was gone, and the Caskeys looked uneasily about them to see who might move into the vacant position. James was eldest, but frail, retiring, and without a calling to leadership. Oscar was Mary-Love's male heir, but the Caskeys were used to a woman at the helm, and Oscar might well have to prove himself fit for such a place. Sister lived away; Grace was completely involved with her life at the Spartanburg girls' school. Queenie wasn't really a Caskey. The burden seemed to be poised above Elinor.

Because the Caskeys began to look upon her as the intuitive choice, they now sought reasons to make her the logical choice as well. She was wife to the man who ran the mill, source of all the Caskey power and prestige. She had status of her own in Perdido. She kept up the largest house in town. She had proved her worth by a willingness to do battle with Mary-Love. Who else had done that except when they hadn't been driven to it in absolute desperation?

It was odd, but Elinor seemed to have changed in recent years. The change had been slower but no less radical than the transformation that James underwent on the day that Mary-Love had died. James Caskey had received more than an intimation of his own mortality: he had seen its very pattern in the wicker casket bathed in colored light. Frances's three-year illness seemed to have accomplished something similar with Elinor. Her single-minded and constant nursing of Frances had almost seemed to suggest that Elinor felt she was capable, alone, of curing her child. As those days of nursing had lengthened into weeks, and the weeks into months, Elinor's resolve to prove her healing prowess had grown. When Frances was finally well again, after three years of suffering, it had been impossible for anyone to say whether the cure had been effected by Elinor's baths, Dr. Benquith's medicine, or by some stray trigger accidentally pulled in Frances's system. Elinor seemed to have been humbled by her daughter's bout with the crippling disease and by her own failure to cure it easily and quickly. During the course of Frances's illness, Elinor had not fought with her mother-in-law. Now that Mary-Love was dead, a chastened Elinor Caskey stood before the family, solemnly prepared to receive the Caskey crown.

The more they all thought of it, the clearer it became that Elinor was to be the new head of the family. There was no actual delegation to inform her of the choice, but there might as well have been. Her opinion was solicited on every matter great and small. Her decision was always acceded to without objection. Her house became the focus of family activity. The hub of the Caskey universe, with a little grinding of gears and spinning of wheels, slipped twenty yards to the west.

Though the Caskeys watched carefully, few alterations in management were apparent. In the first week of mourning for Mary-Love, there was little activity. The Caskeys kept to themselves. Early Haskew had come and gone, leaving behind his wife and tobacco-juice stains on the glossy leaves of Mary-Love's prize camellias. Miriam remained with Sister in Mary-Love's house.

"When are we gone go send for Miriam?" Oscar asked his wife.

"I don't want to uproot her yet," said Elinor. "She's attached to Sister, and when Sister goes back to Chattanooga, that'll be time enough."

"When is Sister planning on going back?"

"She's waiting for the reading of the will, I suppose. I don't know what else could keep her here."

There was some speculation among the Caskeys about the contents of Mary-Love's will. It was assumed in the town that Mary-Love would divide her substantial fortune between her two children, Oscar and Sister. Oscar would at last be rewarded for his many years of service to the mill; Sister would never have to worry about Early's ability to scratch work out of a depressed economy. Doubtless some special provision would be made for Miriam, for the child had been very dear to Mary-Love. Perdido could not imagine that the dead woman had done anything different.

The Caskeys, however, knew to what lengths Mary-Love would go to thwart happiness and dampen expectations. It was not inconceivable, for instance, that she would have left everything to James, who was old and didn't need it; or to Miriam, who was young and couldn't handle it. Elinor, in particular, was anxious for the will to be read. She wanted Oscar to get the money as quickly as possible so that he would be able to purchase Henry Turk's final tract of land. She was fearful another buyer might step forward in the interim. "Just go to Henry, Oscar, and tell him not to sell it to anybody else. Tell him we'll buy it up just as soon as Mary-Love's will is read."

"Elinor, we've just got to wait. We're not sure yet who Mama left her money to. And even if I get half and Sister gets half, it's still gone be a while before the thing's probated. It's gone be six months at least before I see a single dime of Mama's money."

"Then borrow the money from James. We just *can't* let that Escambia County land get away from us."

"Why are you so all fired up to buy land in Florida? We've never seen fit to cross a state line before."

"That's good land over there, Oscar."

"It's just like it is over here, same old trees, same old creeks, same old Perdido River flowing alongside it. Only nobody lives there, and it's hard to get to. Henry Turk never made a crying dime off the land, and that's the reason he's still got it—nobody in his right mind wants that land. Henry was able to get rid of everything but that. And you know if we got it, we'd have to learn all about Florida laws and Florida taxes."

"You'll be sorry if we don't buy it up."

"Why?"

"I know that land," returned Elinor. "Someday it will make us more money than you ever dreamed of."

Oscar was mystified by this remark. As far as he knew, his wife had never crossed over into any part of Escambia County, Florida. How could she know anything of those empty quadrants of pine, ribbed with the creeks and branches that emptied into the lower Perdido?

The will was brief. Two thousand dollars went to Ivey Sapp and Bray Sugarwhite, to build themselves a new house on higher land than Baptist Bottom, and five hundred dollars went to Luvadia Sapp. Seven hundred dollars bought a new window for the Methodist Church attended by the family, and three hundred dollars bought a new baptismal font for the Methodist Church in Baptist Bottom. Ten thousand dollars to the Athenaeum Club established a scholarship for a deserving Perdido girl to attend the University of Alabama.

The Caskeys nodded approval of these small bequests. They showed, everyone thought, a sense of community responsibility in the dead woman.

The bulk of her fortune—her half of the Caskey sawmill and allied industries; the holdings of land and leasing rights; the stocks and bonds; the mortgages and liens upon other properties in Baldwin, Escambia, Monroe, and Washington counties; the savings accounts in the Perdido bank, three Mobile banks, and two Pensacola banks; and the investments in Louisiana and Arkansas—were to be divided equally between her beloved son Oscar and her devoted daughter Elvennia Haskew.

To her granddaughter, Miriam Caskey, Mary-Love left her house, its contents, and the land on which it stood; all her jewels, precious and semiprecious stones—mounted or loose; all silverware and objects of virtu; and the contents of four safe deposit boxes in various banks.

There was enormous relief in the family. Mary-Love had done what everyone thought to be right and proper. She had not sought to perpetuate her animadversions from the grave. The malice of her cloying love apparently had been dampened when she had contemplated her own death in the writing of her testament.

Miriam was sixteen, but she seemed grown-up. And she thought she had reason to seem so. After all, she was an heiress in her own right. She had cases of jewels in her room, and she had safety-deposit boxes of diamonds and rubies and sapphires in four different banks in Mobile. She was no one's daughter. Mary-Love had died and left her as alone as if she had been abandoned in the midst of the pine forest. She didn't belong to her parents, for they had given her up when she was a baby. Despite their proximity during the intervening years, they remained little more than strangers. They were rather like cousins, once or twice removed, whom one didn't particularly care for, though they bore one's name and one's likeness. She wasn't Sister's either, though once she had been. Sister had gone off and married Early Haskew, whom Miriam deprecated for his coarse country ways and his chewing tobacco.

Sister and Miriam sat at the supper table together a few hours after the will was read. Sister had helped raise Miriam when she was a baby, but after Sister's marriage, Miriam had become Mary-Love's child alone. Sister and Miriam had not exactly become strangers, but there was now a certain distance between them.

"It's funny," said Miriam.

"What is?"

"To think that this whole house is mine now, and everything in it."

"I'm glad Mama left it to you," said Sister. "That way you can sell it and put some money in the bank. That'll send you to school."

"I don't intend to sell it."

Sister looked up, surprised. "You're gone let it sit here empty? You shouldn't, you know. Rats take up in empty houses. Squirrels will break in through the roof."

"I'm gone live here," said Miriam.

Sister was more surprised than ever. "You're not coming back to Chattanooga with me?"

"I hate Chattanooga."

"You've never even been there. What do you *think* you'd hate about it?"

"Everything."

"That's no answer."

"Do you really want an answer, Sister?"

"Yes, of course I do."

"I wouldn't be comfortable," said Miriam.

"Comfortable?"

"Around Early."

"You don't like Early?"

"I'm not comfortable around him, that's all. He's too...country. I'm not used to being around country people."

Sister flushed. "That school you go to is *filled* with boys and girls who are a lot more country than Early."

"But I don't have to live with them."

Miriam and Sister then passed plates around for second helpings. Ivey came out of the kitchen and poured more iced tea.

"Ivey's already said she would stay on with me."

"Yes, ma'am," said Ivey to Sister. "I did say it."

Sister shook her head. "What's your mama gone say?"

"You mean Elinor?"

"Yes, of course I mean Elinor. If I go off back to Chattanooga and don't take you with me, Elinor's gone say that you got to move in with her and Oscar over there."

"I wouldn't move in with them if they threw a rope over my neck and *dragged* me across the yard."

"Elinor might do it. Elinor wants you back. She's spoken to me about it."

"What did she say?"

"She said, 'Sister, don't try to take Miriam back to Chattanooga, because I want her over here with me.'"

"She can't have me!"

"You're her *daughter,* Miriam. That's what it comes down to."

They were silent for a while longer. Ivey cleared

159

away and brought out dessert. It was Boston cream pie, Sister's favorite.

"I don't want to go to Chattanooga," said Miriam to Ivey.

"No, I know you don't," said Ivey in mild confirmation.

"And I certainly don't want to move in with Elinor and Oscar."

"No, ma'am, I *know* you don't want to do that."

"I want to stay right in this house."

"You love this house," said Ivey with pride. "Miss Mary-Love wanted you to have it to live in."

"Then what do I do? How do I get to stay on here?" Miriam looked to the black woman for an answer. Sister, as if she knew exactly what that answer was going to be, continued eating her pie.

"Miss Miriam, why don't you ask Sister to stay on here with you?"

Miriam looked surprised. "But what about Early?"

"Mr. Early's got his jobs here, there, everywhere," said Ivey. "Sister, you want another piece of pie?"

"I sure do."

"Sister," said Miriam, "will you stay on here with me? Be my mama?"

Sister dug into the second piece of pie. "Let me think about it, Miriam. Let me put that idea under my pillow."

Next morning at breakfast, the first thing Miriam said to Sister was: "Did you decide?"

"No, and I don't want to be pestered about this, either. You have no right to ask me to leave Early just so you can do what you want."

"Then you're leaving?"

"Not yet."

"When?"

"I said that I don't want to be pestered about this."

"When can I ask you again if you've made up your mind?"

160

"Never."

"Then what do I say to Elinor when she comes over here and wants to carry me off?"

"I'll deal with your mother, Miriam. Just stop asking me about it."

Miriam said no more. And her evil day was postponed, because Sister did not return to Chattanooga. She remained in Perdido a week beyond the reading of the will, then two weeks, then a month. The girl, lived, however, in continual suspense, because Sister never would say how long she intended to remain in the house that had been deeded to Miriam.

Next door, Oscar worried. He thought it was time for Sister to return home, and for Miriam to move into the front room. He mentioned his misgivings to Elinor, who said, "Leave it alone, Oscar. Don't push things."

"What do you mean, Elinor? What is there to push? Is there something you know about that you're not telling me?"

"Nobody's told me anything. If I were you, though, I'd just leave Sister and Miriam alone for the time being."

"I have," protested Oscar. "And now I just want to know how long this 'time being' is going to go on. Do you know?"

"I do not."

"I'm gone have to go over there."

Elinor didn't waste any more words in an attempt to dissuade her husband, and that evening he knocked on the front door of his daughter's house. Sister let him in. He hadn't been inside the house for five years. "Sister, can I speak to Miriam for a minute?"

"Of course, Oscar. Let me go upstairs and get her."

In a few minutes, Miriam came down alone. "Hello, Oscar," she said, pointedly eschewing the appellation "Father."

"Hello, honey. I came over because I thought there were a few things we ought to talk about."

"All right," said Miriam, seating herself in the mahogany platform rocker which her grandmother had often occupied. Oscar sat in a corner of the blue sofa, where he had so often been placed as a child.

"Miriam, darling," Oscar began, "your mama and I need to figure out what's going to become of you."

"How do you mean?"

"Where you're going to go and what you're going to do, now that Mama's dead."

"I'm not going to do anything," Miriam replied calmly. "I'm not going to go anywhere."

"You mean you don't want to come over and live with your mama and Frances and me?"

"No, sir. I have my own room here, and I don't want to leave."

"You'd have your own room next door. Elinor says you could have the front room."

"I don't want that room—or any room in that house. I just want to stay here. This is my house. Grandmama left it to me because she wanted me to live here. And that's exactly what I intend to do."

"But what happens when Sister goes back to Chattanooga? What would people in this town think if they heard I was allowing a sixteen-year-old girl to live all by herself in a big house like this?"

"They could think whatever they wanted," returned Miriam. "What do I care what people think? I don't intend to leave, and nobody can make me."

"Your mama and I could make you," said Oscar. "We're your parents."

Miriam looked directly at her father. "I suppose you could make me. I suppose you could rope me to the bed. I suppose you could stick food down my throat till I swallowed it."

"You don't want to live with us?" Oscar asked his daughter, plaintively.

"Of course, I don't."

"Why not?"

"You didn't want me when I was born. And now it's too late."

For a few moments, her father sat stunned.

"That was…sixteen years ago…darling!" Oscar faltered when he had recovered himself. "And Mama wanted a little girl of her own. You're not sorry we gave you to Mama, are you?"

Miriam made no reply.

"You cain't still be upset about that, not after all these years. You know how much your grandmama loved you. You know how happy you were with Sister and Mama. We would never have let you go if we hadn't thought you were gone be happy as the day is long."

Miriam looked at her father impassively and said nothing.

"Miriam, you are only sixteen years old. You cain't tell me what to do and expect me to hop to it." This injunction carried no conviction in Oscar's mouth.

"I'm not trying to tell you what to do, Oscar. I'm just telling you what I'm *not* gone do. And what I'm *not* gone do is leave this house, at least not of my own free will. You can get Mr. Key down here and have him throw me in jail for not doing what you tell me to do, or you can get Zaddie to tie me up with clothesline and put me in a croker sack and carry me over there on a cane pole, but that's about the only way you will get me inside that house."

"It hurts me to hear you speak like this, darling!"

Miriam said nothing.

"I'm gone send Elinor over here to talk to you. She's gone have to try to talk some sense into your head about all this. You are so upset about Mama that you're plumb not thinking straight."

"If Elinor comes over here…"

"Yes?"

"…just tell her to make sure she brings me the rings she stole off Grandmama's fingers. Otherwise, I'm not gone speak to her."

Oscar sank deeper into the corner of the blue sofa where he had so often been placed as a child to listen to his mother's pronouncements. He looked at his daughter Miriam as he had looked at Mary-Love Caskey in that far-off time. In his daughter, who was so great a stranger to him, he saw much of his mother. He understood for the first time that Miriam bore as much animosity toward Elinor as Mary-Love had. Oscar didn't know what was to come of all this, but he now knew that Miriam would never take up residence in his house.

Miriam sedately rocked beneath the red-shaded lamp, her thick, carefully brushed hair falling across her face and shadowing her expression. She did not appear to concern herself overmuch with this discussion of her future. She seemed only politely to conceal her impatience with her father to get on with whatever it was he had come to say.

Seeing his daughter thus, Oscar decided to say no more. Miriam might be only sixteen, but Oscar decided that he would be very surprised if she did not get her own way. He wondered if Elinor had yet realized to what extent Miriam was prepared to take her grandmother's place.

CHAPTER 42

The Linen Closet

Sister remained on in Perdido through the winter. There was speculation as to why she had deserted her husband in that manner. Early Haskew came to town for Christmas, but his visit was strained. He was gone again by New Year's. Perdido, and all the Caskeys—including Miriam herself—assumed that it was on Miriam's account that Sister stayed. Sister was sacrificing her own marriage at the whim of that spoiled girl, everyone thought. She elected to remain in Perdido in a house of mourning for the wholly inadequate reason that Miriam Caskey didn't want to move twenty yards to the west and take up residence in her parents' home.

No one ever brought this up to Sister Haskew directly. No one had the right. It was Sister's prerogative to throw her marriage away for Miriam's sake, as surely as it had been her right to marry against her mother's wishes.

Sister actually remained in Perdido, however, not

for Miriam's sake but for her own. Sister hid behind the sacrificial theory of her conduct, rather than to admit—even to the members of her own family— that she had made a mistake in her choice of husbands.

In thirteen years of marriage, Early Haskew had coarsened. During their courtship, Early had been a resident in Mary-Love's house, and in those prosperous surroundings, he had been on his best behavior. After he and Sister were married, left Perdido, and began living on Early's meager and uncertain earnings, his country ways reasserted themselves. He chewed tobacco, a habit that Sister despised as much as did Miriam, though she would never have admitted it. And she never had grown accustomed to his eating peas off a knife. His habitual clumsiness deteriorated into slovenliness. His body grew fat and shapeless. He would take a biscuit, punch a hole in it with his forefinger, fill the hole with molasses, and then swallow the whole thing in one gulp. Pillowcases smelled of the rancid oil he used on his hair.

Early's friends were even coarser than he, so coarse that Sister wouldn't even allow them inside the house, but made them, on visits, remain on the front porch. They lived in a run-down section of Chattanooga, and Sister couldn't afford more than a woman who boiled linen. She had to do ironing herself. One day she came home from the grocery and discovered Early and two of his cronies lifting a Coca-Cola vending machine onto their front porch.

Early bred pit bull terriers for fighting, and seemed to care about nothing but those damned dogs—Sister never thought of them except in those words. He insisted on her rising twice each night to feed new litters out of a baby bottle. When the dogs weren't feeding they were yelping, and Sister got no sleep between-times. Early's coarseness finally wore her down. Now in Perdido, she was getting worn down by having constantly to defend her husband against that charge.

When Sister came into her inheritance, she at first had a vision of herself returning to Tennessee and buying a decent house, purchasing a new wardrobe for Early, encouraging him to drop his ne'er-do-well friends and his reprehensible pastimes, and raising him to a level of gentility commensurate with her own. This she thought was possible, yet it was a task she did not look forward to with relish. Early seemed too set in his ways, too far along the path in which he had been born. The real Early Haskew, Sister thought, was the Early Haskew who went about the house without a shirt and trained puppies to viciousness with slaps and red meat, the one who chewed tobacco and snored loud enough to wake all creation. The man she had met and married in 1922 had been a man caught then in a brief and deceptive stage of development, like one of his own handsome pups that would soon grow into a snarling vicious brute.

Mary-Love, Sister remembered, had known the change would come, and she had warned her. Sister herself might have foretold it, for there were many similar men around Perdido. Sister's marriage had been as much an act of defiance toward her mother as it had been an attraction toward Early. Early's attraction faded quickly for Sister, while her need to defy her mother continued strong and unabated till the day of Mary-Love's death—when it suddenly evaporated. With it went any good reason Sister had to return to the white frame house in the run-down section of Chattanooga, the pit bull pups, or Early Haskew.

She seized upon Miriam's desire to remain in Mary-Love's house as an excuse not to return to Tennessee. In using this as a disguise for her real motive, she was being craftier than her mother had ever been. Everyone thought that Sister's remaining in Perdido was a great sacrifice; no one for one moment suspected that she dreaded the day when Miriam would go off to college or marry. Then Sister would have to announce her total disgust with Early Haskew.

Though she was only a few months liberated from her bed and wheelchair, the three years of crippling illness Frances had suffered were a misty time—garbled, drowsy, and leaden. She had grown in those missing years—not much, it was true—but enough to now make her unfamiliar with her body. Prior to that terrible time she had been a child, with a child's fears. Now she was nearly an adult; the childish fears were put behind her.

On the night of her return from the journey to Chicago, when Mary-Love lay in the casket in the front parlor, Frances slept in her own room. Elinor and Oscar had considered that their daughter might be terrified of sleeping in a house in which her grandmother's body lay, but Frances told them that there was no need for her to bother James or Queenie with her presence that night. She said this not because she no longer was afraid, but so that she might test the extent to which those fears remained with her. It had been no surprise to Frances that her grandmother had died in the front room.

After the funeral, as Zaddie helped her unpack her traveling clothes and all the new little treasures that James and Queenie had purchased for her, Frances could perceive no alteration in the atmosphere of the house because of the death in the front room. She even thought to herself, *Grandmama died in the next room*, but she didn't shake. She smelled the air and detected no odor of death or of her own fear. She stood in the hallway and looked down at the door of the front room. Still the fear didn't come. She approached the door and touched the handle gingerly—no electricity, no fear.

She turned the knob and pushed the door open. It

swung wide and Frances stood on the threshold of the room, feeling nothing.

She looked into the room. She smelled nothing but the dried lavender that had been placed in a bowl on a table beside the bed.

Daringly, she stepped far enough into the room to be able to push the door shut behind her.

She looked at the closet door, and she said to herself, *Mama says Grandmama died of a fever. Sister says Grandmama would have lived if only Daddy had put her in the hospital. But I know that Grandmama was killed by whatever it is that lives in that closet.*

The closet door didn't open. Frances didn't die. "I am fifteen years old," she said aloud, "and I'm not afraid of closets that are filled with feathers and leather and fur."

Months passed, and Frances turned sixteen. She had never been close to her grandmother and had not seen her at all during her illness. She did not often think of her dead, and sometimes she actually forgot, when she looked out her bedroom window at Mary-Love's house, that Mary-Love had died the previous summer. Frances checked—as she had as a child—to see if her grandmother were sitting in her rocker by her bedroom window.

An Italian stone cutter in Mobile carved Mary-Love's monument in Georgia marble. It was raised seven months after her death. All the Caskeys attended the brief, informal ceremony. Miriam, Queenie, and Frances laid flowers. Frances once again thought, *Grandmama died in the front room.*

That night she fell asleep immediately and did not dream. And a short time later she was just as immediately awakened; not by any sound, but by a sense that something was horribly wrong.

Her room was suffused with a weak, bluish-white light. It shone through the window, as definite as though a streetlamp had been raised in the vicinity of her dead grandmother's house. She had no idea what the source of that strange illumination might be, but she stared with terror at the white sheer curtains over the window. She dared not rise to look out. She turned to the other window, that opened onto the screened sleeping porch. The porch, too, was illuminated by the glow, though it wasn't as strong as in her own room.

Then quite suddenly and with alarm, she remembered the light which had filled the front closet, and afterwards the entire front room, on the night that Carl Strickland had fired on them from the levee. Frances had been very young then, and all incidents that occurred prior to her long bout with illness were vague and dreamlike. But this light she recognized and remembered. It had been no dream then; it was no dream now.

It wasn't that unnatural light that raised fear in Frances's soul. Without her willing it, her head turned to look at the door that opened onto the narrow linen corridor that separated her room from the front room. She knew something had found its way into that narrow closed hallway. It was there, and she knew it wasn't a person. It wasn't her mother. It wasn't her father. It wasn't Zaddie. Whatever lived and hid in the front room closet had gotten out of the closet, roamed over the front room, opened the door of the linen corridor, and had slunk down it. Now it waited on the other side of the door.

It wasn't her grandmother's ghost, but Frances knew that it was somehow connected with the raising of the marble stone over her grandmother's grave.

She lay terrified in her bed. The crippling arthritis seemed to have returned to her hands and feet. She tried to imagine what the thing on the other side of the door was like, but couldn't. She knew it was the color of the light outside, and that if she looked to the door again, she would see the light pouring through the crack beneath it. *That* was where the outside light was coming from. The front room was so bright that the light shone out of the windows, and that's what she was seeing through the curtains. The passage to the front room was filled with even brighter light, because whatever it was, was there, just behind her door. It had no outline that Frances's unwilling imagination could pin down because that outline shifted. She thought of a little boy wearing overalls with bulging pockets. She thought of a hunchbacked man crouching with his mouth open wide. She thought of a handsome, smiling woman with a rope of black pearls about her neck, holding a pound cake on a platter. Images faded into others and between them were shapeless things or shapes she couldn't recognize: fishy things, froggy things, snaky things, things with bulging eyes and webbed hands and shining rubbery skin. The images changed as quickly as shadows that passed across the windows of a train traveling through a sunlit forest. Frances lay with her eyes tight closed for she knew not how long.

Hoping that her fear had its basis only in her mind, she tried to think of something else. If she wasn't close to sleep, she nevertheless seemed close to dreaming. In that half-dream she began to remember the years of her illness. It hadn't been all that long before, but the memories of that buried period of time were like those of earliest childhood, or the fugitive memories of a former existence. As Frances lay in her bed with her eyes tightly shut, trying to will out of existence the thing in the linen closet, she suddenly remembered two things about her illness, one of them impossible, the other improbable.

The first—the impossible—memory was of the thrice-daily baths she had received. At other, more conscious times, she had been able to recall vividly the moment that she was lifted out of the bathtub by her mother. But now—and the sensate memory was sharp despite the impossibility of the thing—

171

her conviction was that during those baths she had always been *fully immersed,* so that she had spent five or six hours a day with her entire body—including her head—beneath the water's surface.

The second memory—impossible too—was of a child, a little boy, who kept her company at night while her mother was asleep. He was younger than Malcolm, but older than Danjo. He was pale and unhappy, and used to pull on Frances's arm, wanting her to play games with him. She never remembered how he came to be in the room with her, but she knew that when he left, he always disappeared into the short passage that led to the front room.

That's who's in the passage now.

She opened her eyes suddenly, and stared at the door. Then audible words were on her lips, and she spoke them automatically, without realizing that she spoke: "Come on in, John Robert."

She didn't know any John Robert.

There was a change behind the door, a kind of quiver or shudder.

The thing in the corridor had up to now been still. Frances knew the fluidity of its images and aspects had all been in her mind. The thing itself had sat immobile on the other side of the door.

Now its arm reached out toward the knob.

Frances leaped out of bed, flew past the blowing curtains shining bluish-white, and threw herself against the door to the linen corridor.

"No!" she cried, "I don't want you!"

Her feet glowed in the light that poured from beneath the door. She turned the key in the lock and immediately stumbled back, her eyes closed.

When she opened her eyes, she could no longer see the light. Her room was dark. She went to the window and looked out. All was still and black. The curtain sheers blew against her face.

She returned to her bed. Nothing was in the corridor. She fell asleep without even wondering if she could do so.

When she woke in the morning, she knew that all she had felt and seen and known had not been a dream brought on by the melancholy excitement of the day. Frances Caskey knew for certain that whatever it was that previously had been confined to the misshapen closet had somehow been allowed to range freely. What was worse was Frances's conviction that some time she would again say, "Come in, John Robert," and not reach the door in time to lock it.

"Michael McDowell's best book yet...He is one of the best writers of horror in this country."
—Peter Straub

MICHAEL McDOWELL'S
CONTINUING SAGA OF THE CASKEY FAMILY.
BLACKWATER

BLACKWATER, an epic novel of horror, will appear serially for six months beginning in January 1983 with completion in June. Michael McDowell, described by Stephen King as "the finest writer of paperback originals in America," is at the height of his storytelling prowess as he tells of the powers exerted by the mysterious Elinor Dammert over the citizens of Perdido, Alabama. Her ghastly, inexplicable ability to use water to gain her hideous ends is a recurring and mystifying pattern.

THE FLOOD (January)   THE WAR (April)
THE LEVEE (February)   THE FORTUNE (May)
THE HOUSE (March)   RAIN (June)